Thanks to Thalie and the entire Geslepen Potloden studio.

MAX DE RADIGUÈS

STIG & TILDE

LEADER OF THE PACK

NOBROW

London | New York

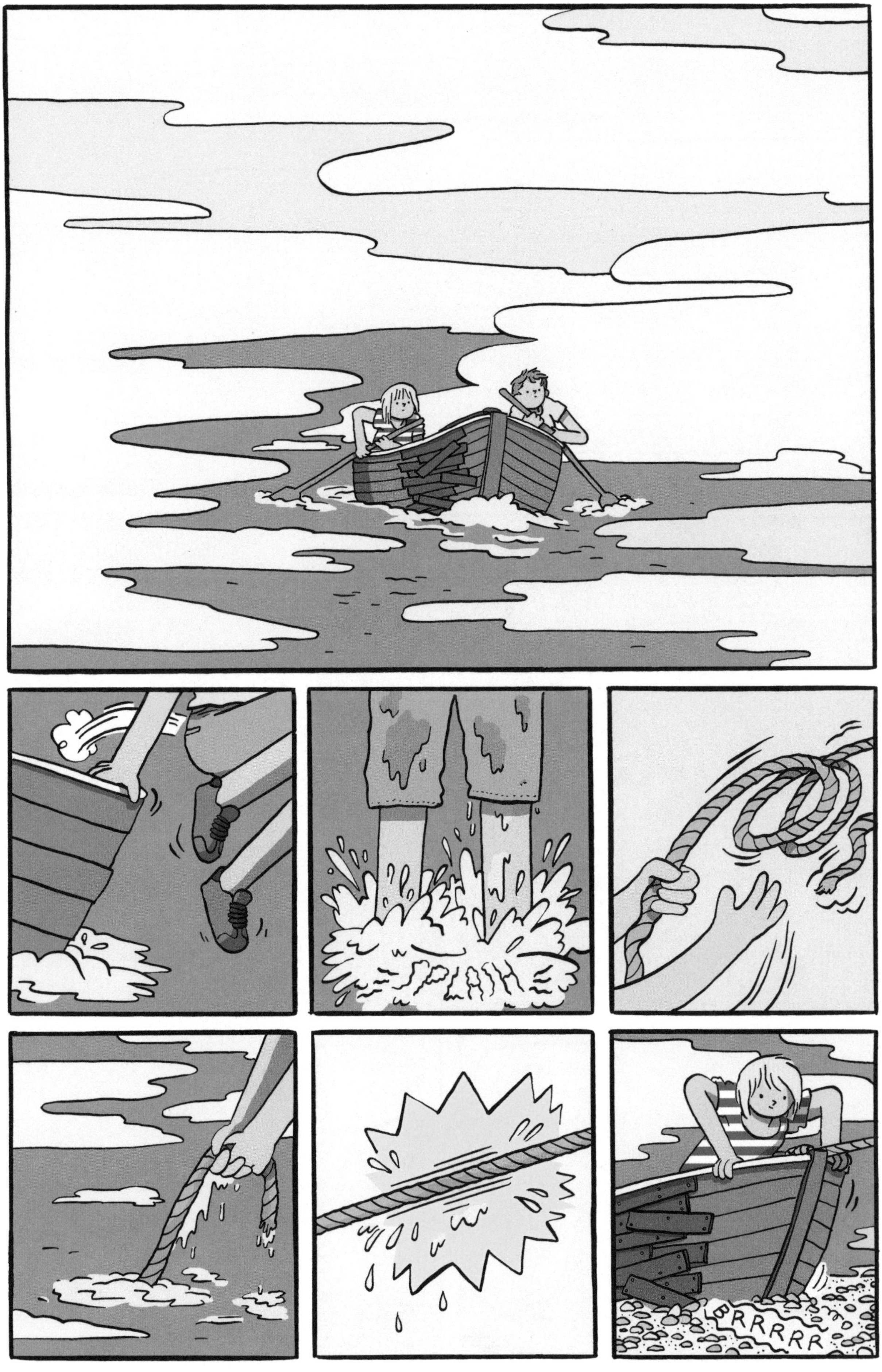
SPLASH
BRRRRRR

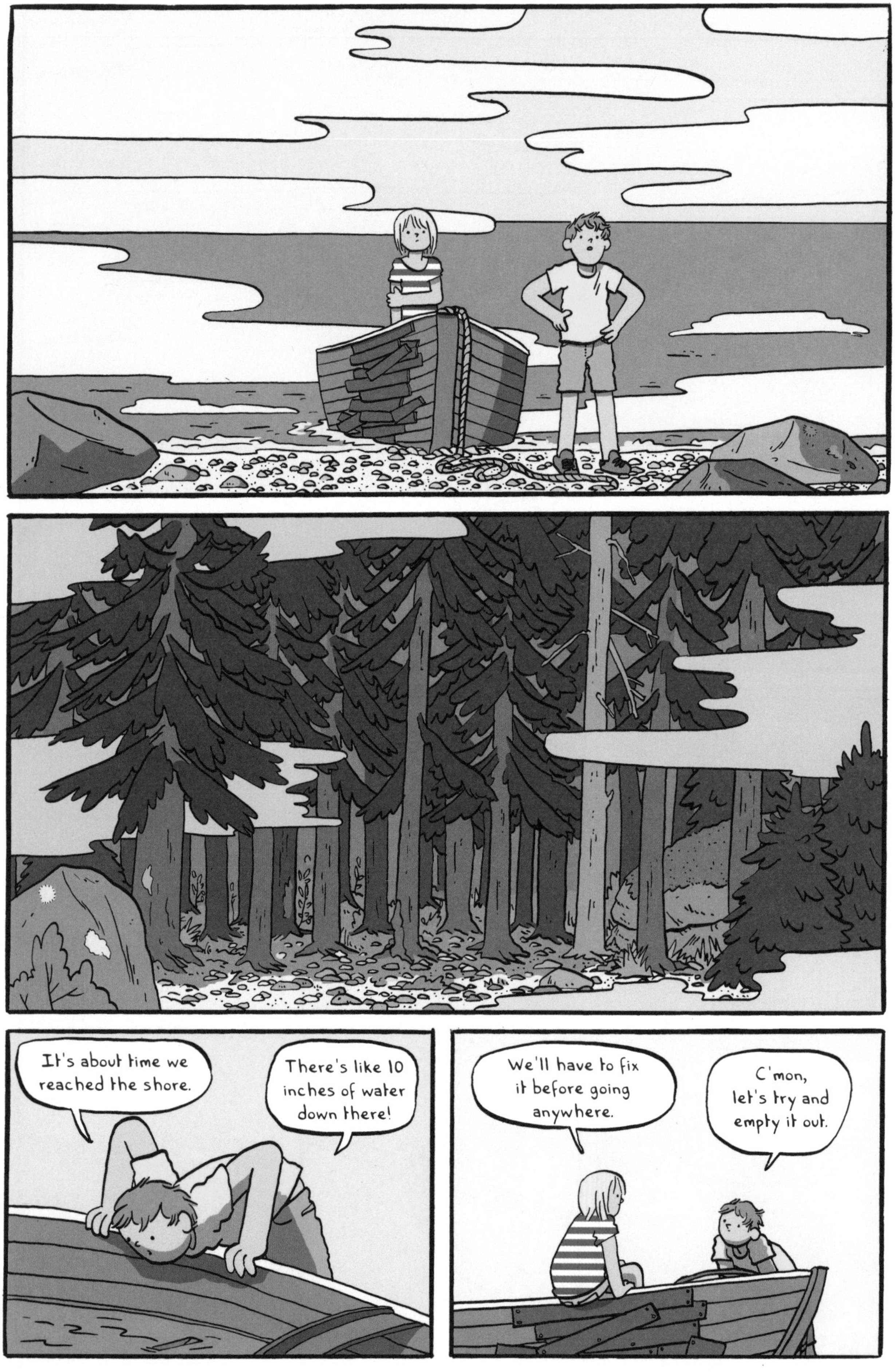
It's about time we reached the shore.
There's like 10 inches of water down there!
We'll have to fix it before going anywhere.
C'mon, let's try and empty it out.

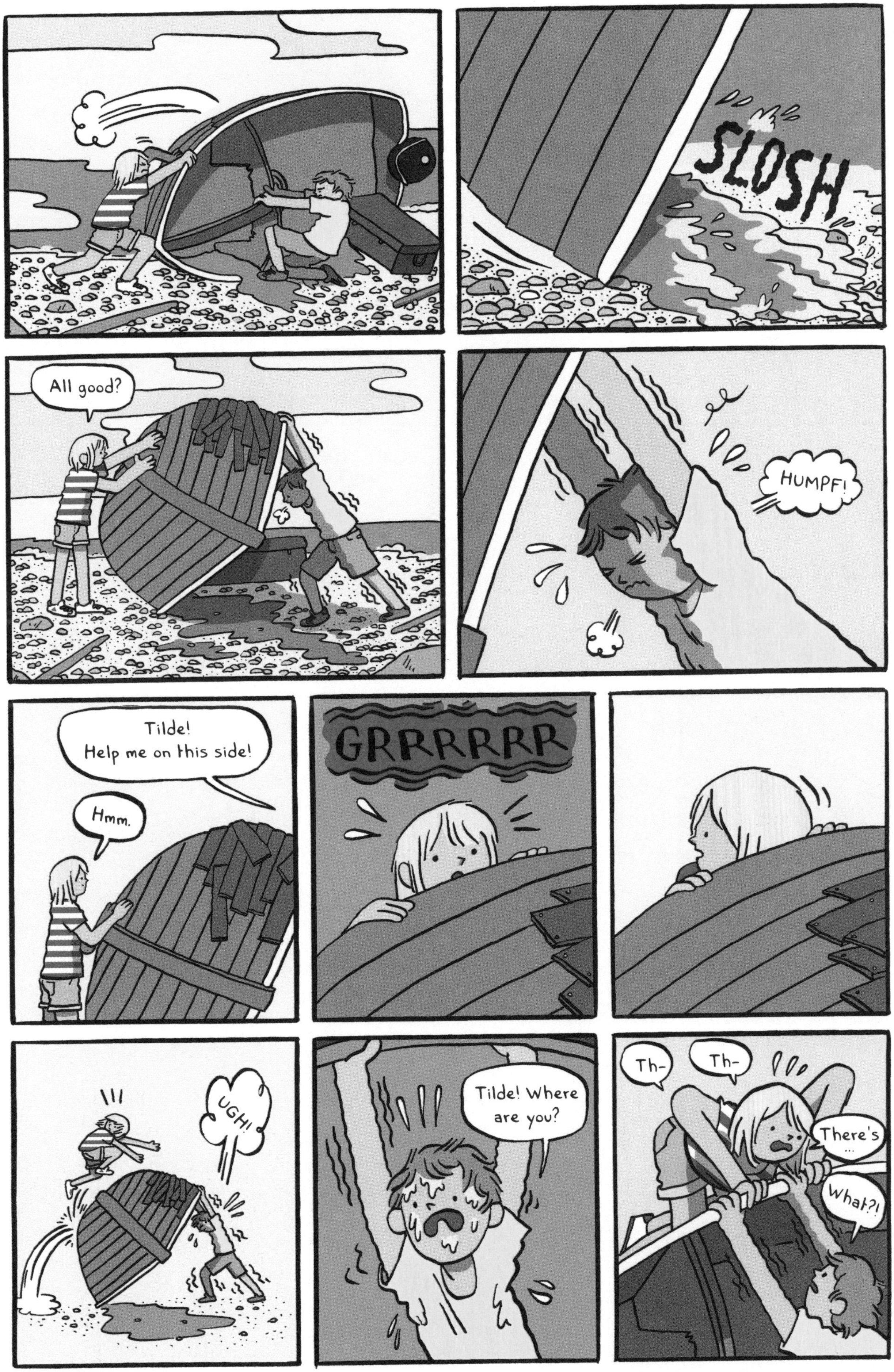
SLOSH
All good?
HUMPF!
Tilde! Help me on this side!
Hmm.
GRRRRRR
UGH!
Tilde! Where are you?
Th-
Th-
There's ...
What?!

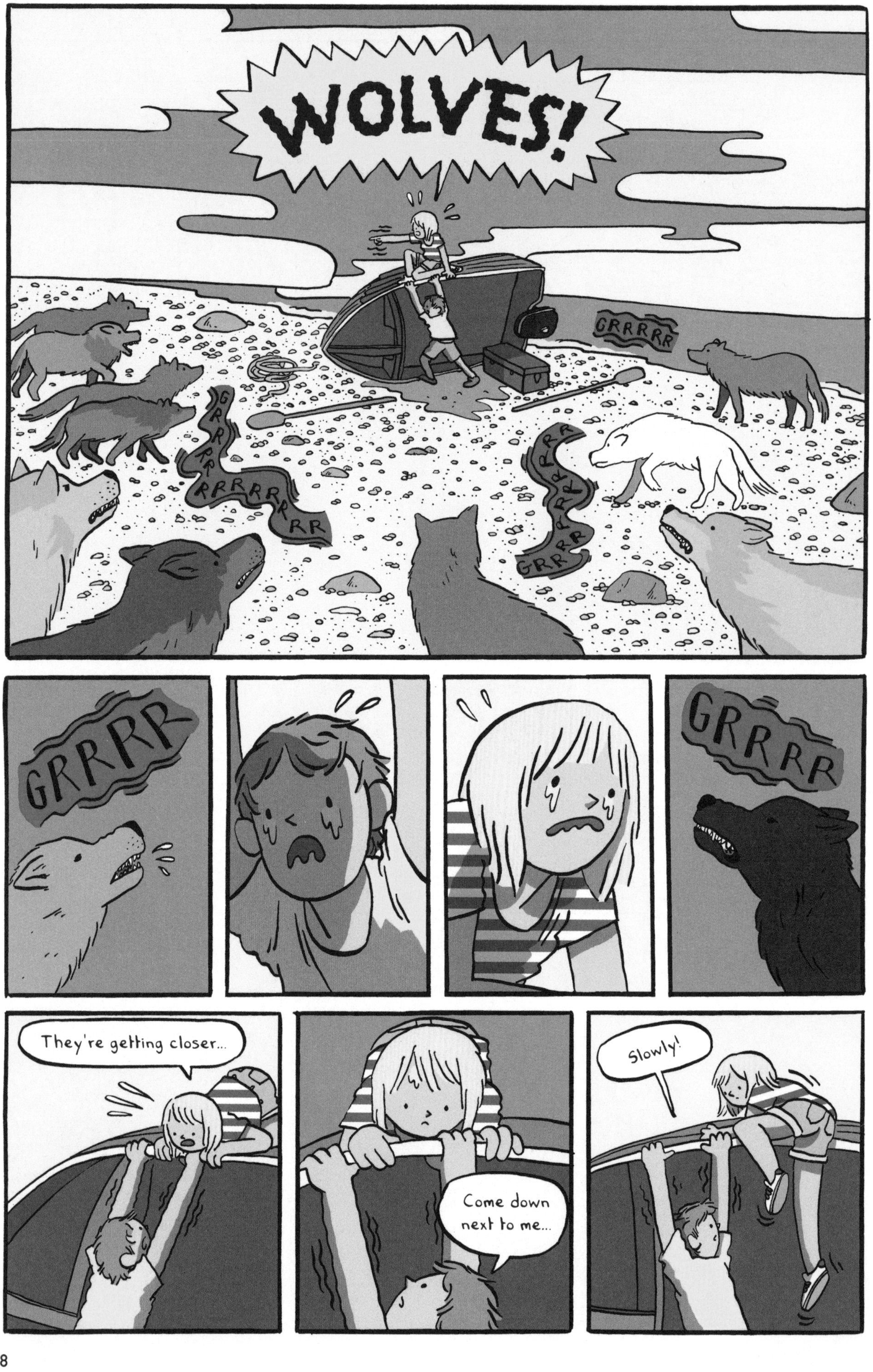
WOLVES!
GRRRR
GRRRR
They're getting closer...
Come down next to me...
Slowly!

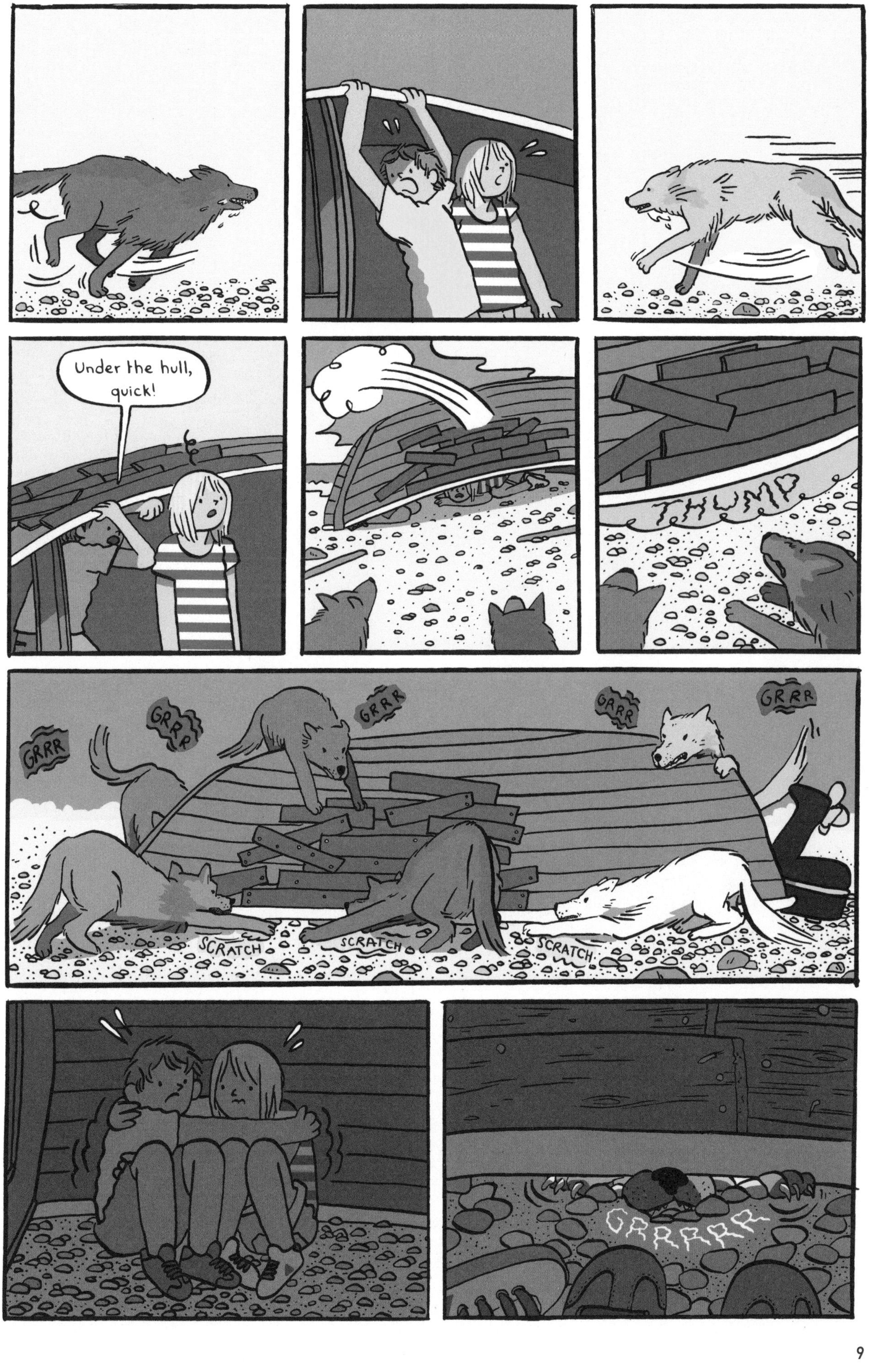
Under the hull, quick!
THUMP
GRRR
GRRR
GRRR
GRRR
GRRR
SCRATCH
SCRATCH
SCRATCH
GRRRRR

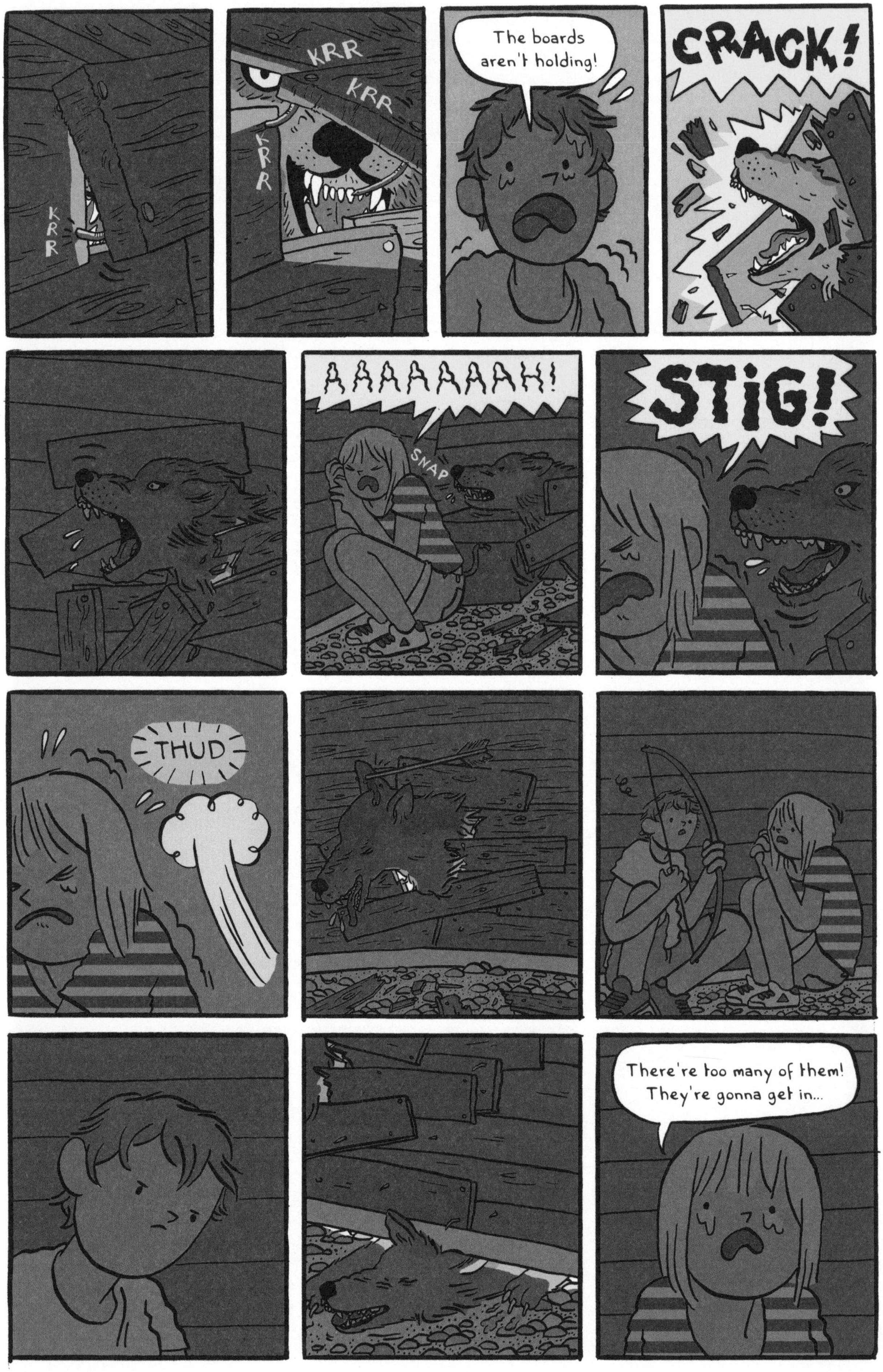
KRR
KRR
KRR
KRR
KRR
The boards aren't holding!
CRACK!
AAAAAAAH!
SNAP
STIG!
THUD
There're too many of them! They're gonna get in...

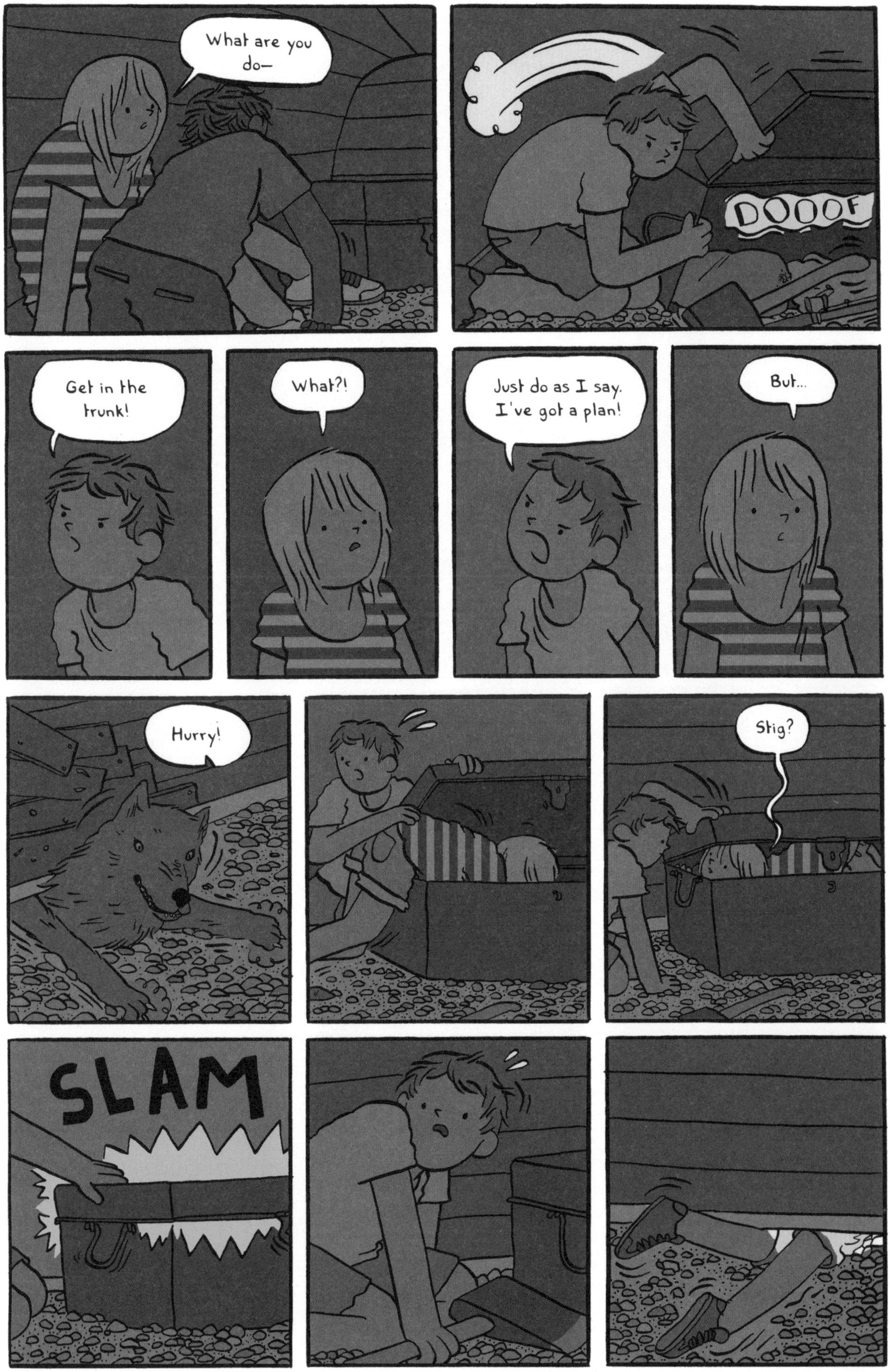
What are you do—
DOOOF
Get in the trunk!
What?!
Just do as I say. I've got a plan!
But...
Hurry!
Stig?
SLAM

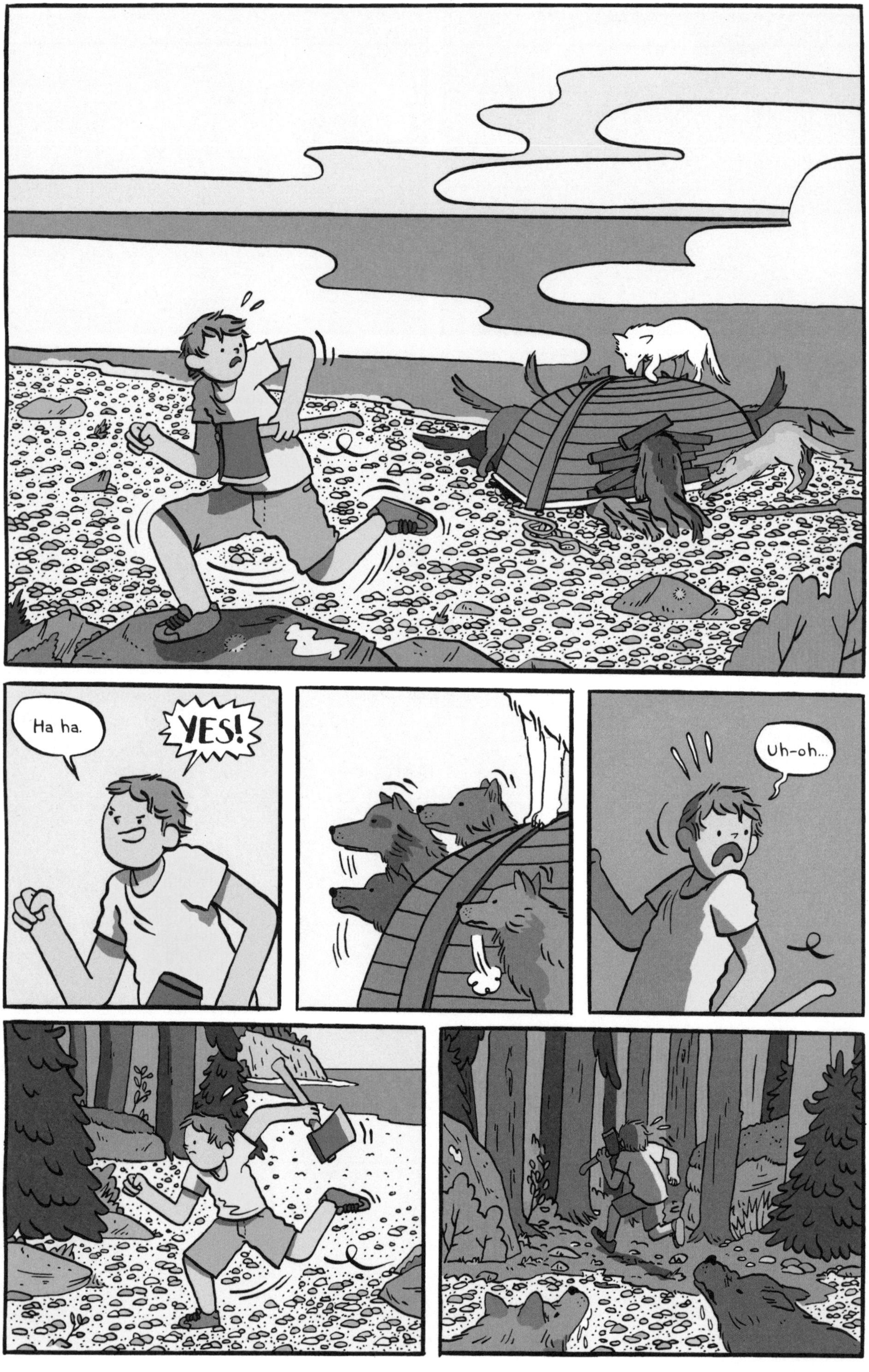
Ha ha.
YES!
Uh-oh...

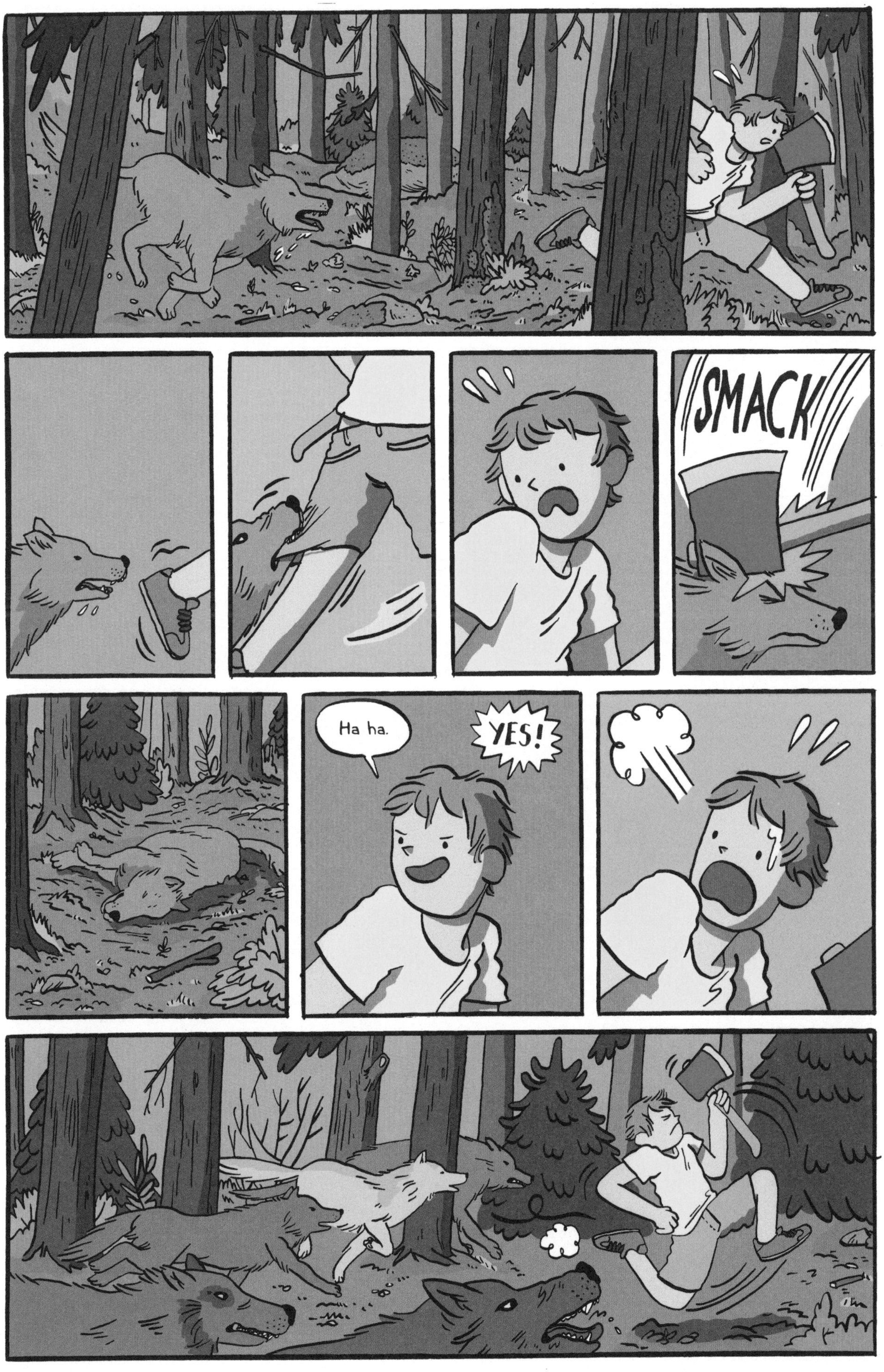
SMACK
Ha ha.
YES!

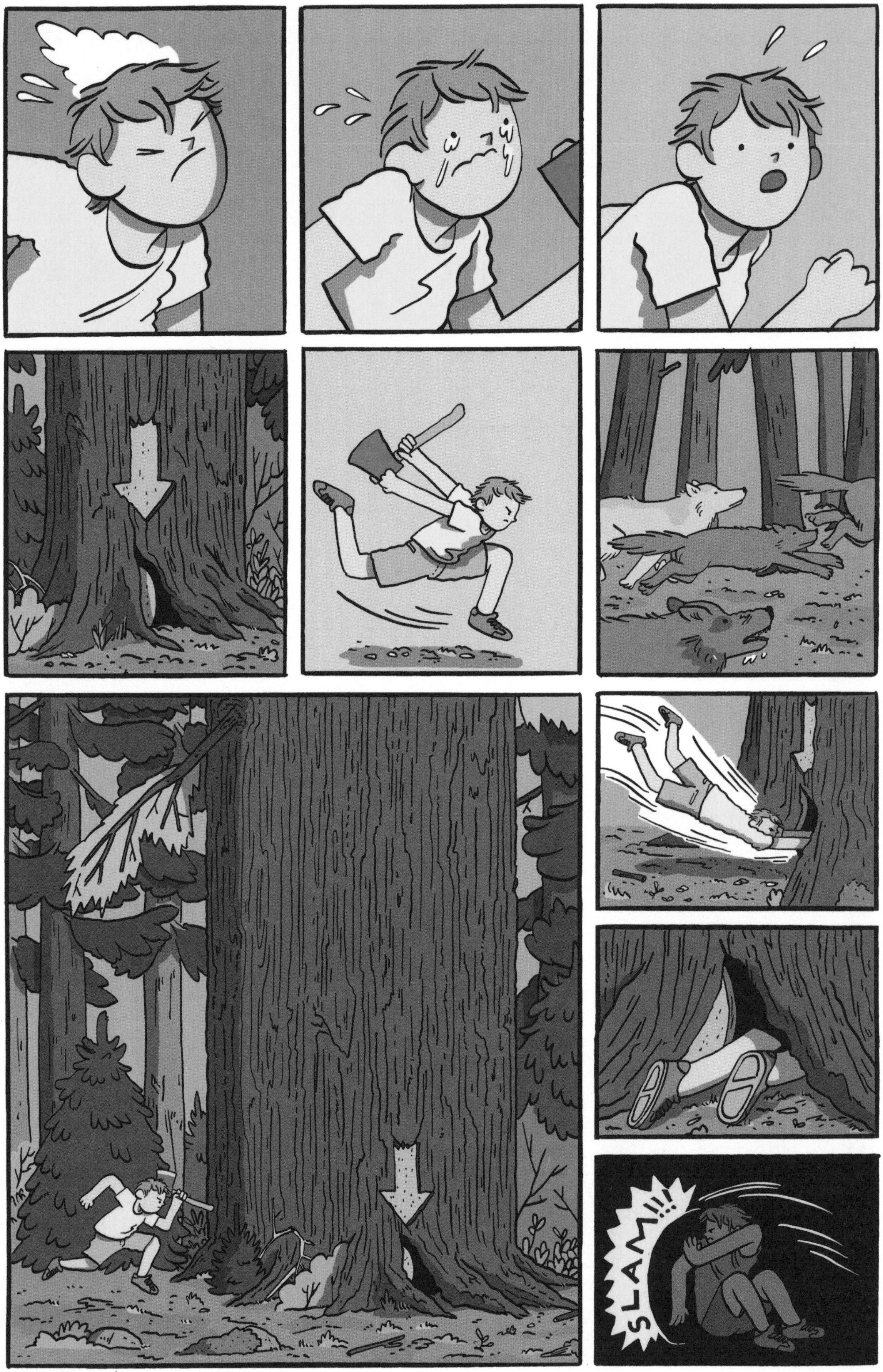
SLAM!!!

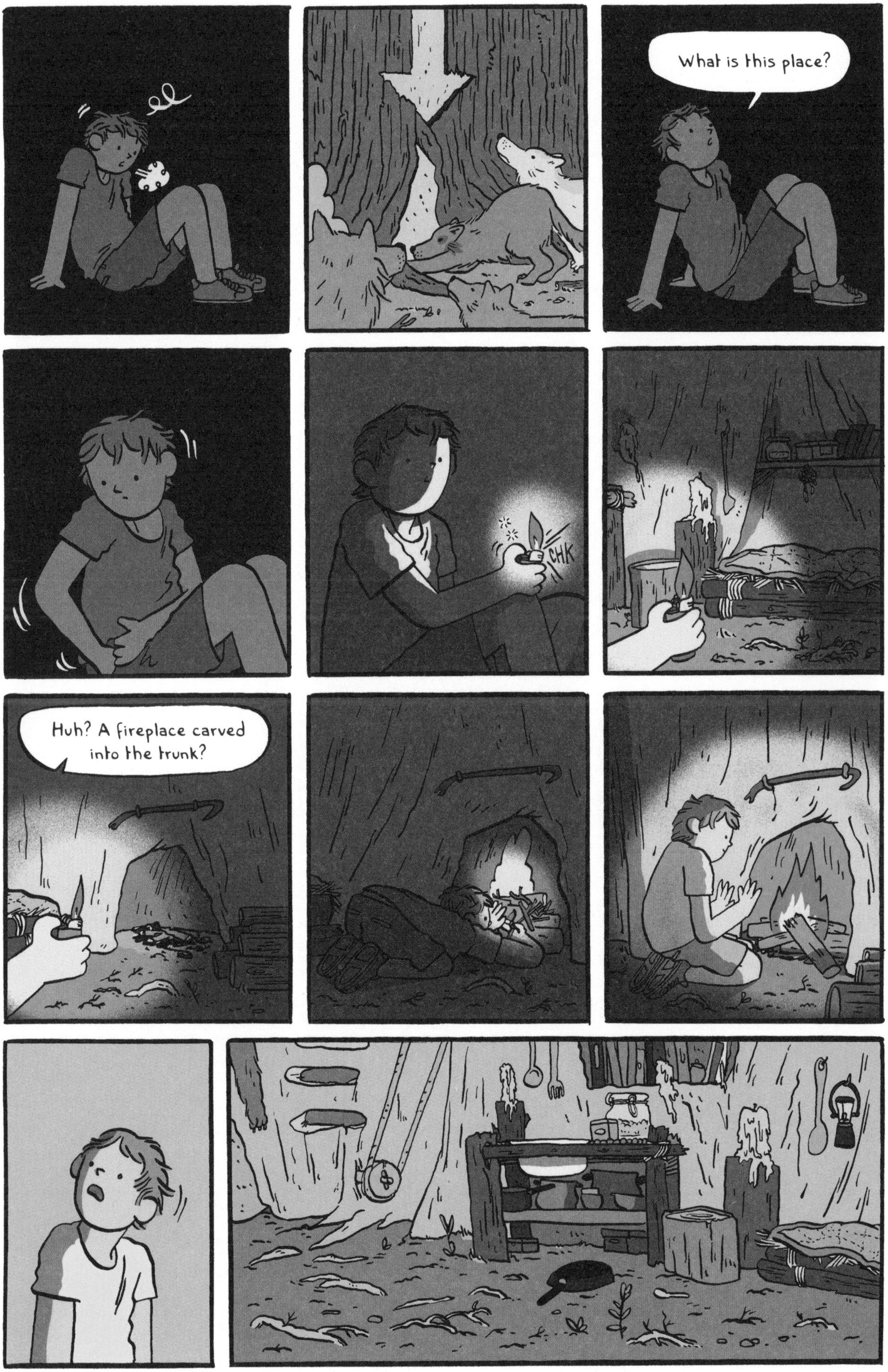
What is this place?
CHK
Huh? A fireplace carved into the trunk?

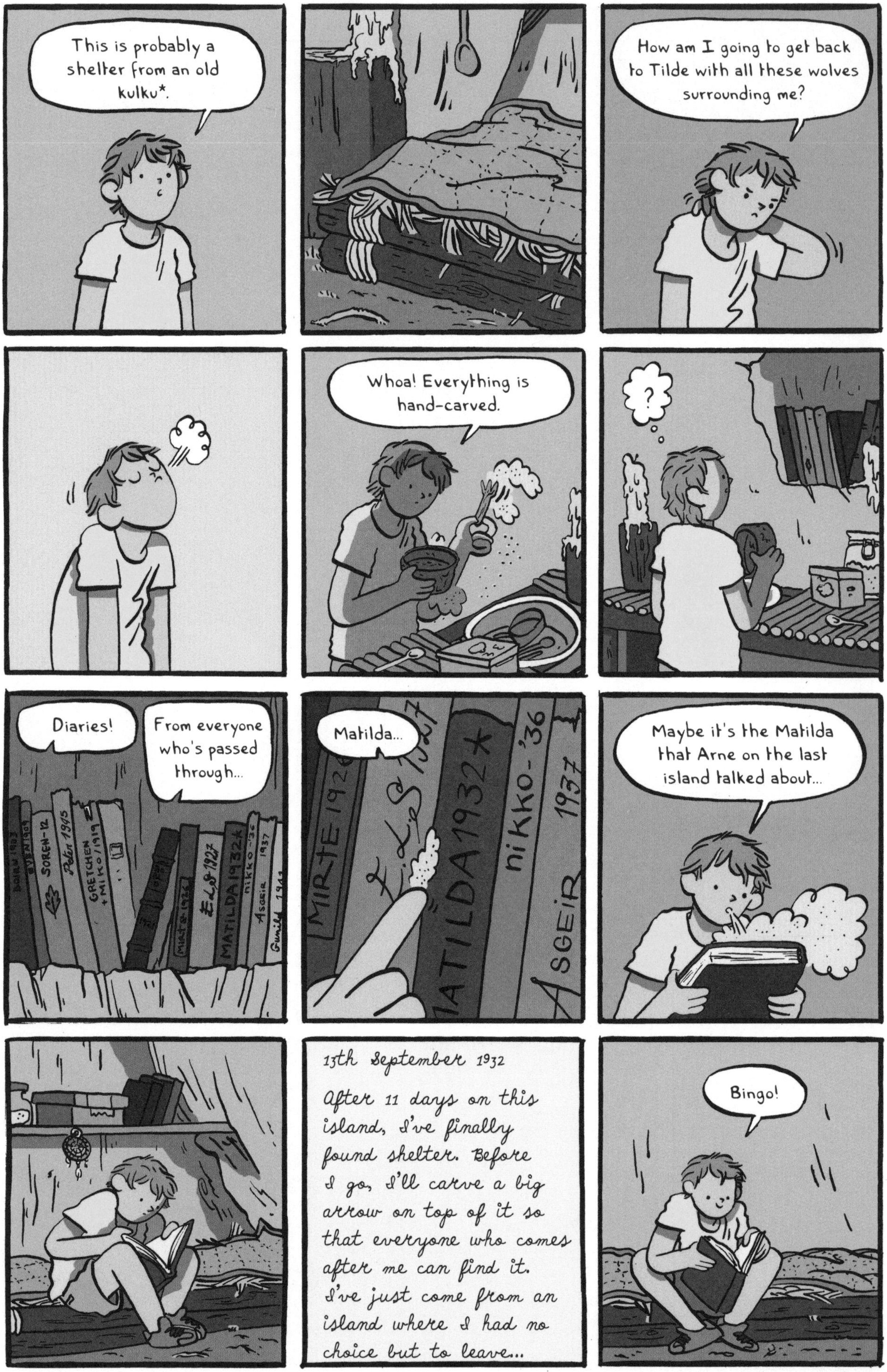
This is probably a shelter from an old kulku*.
How am I going to get back to Tilde with all these wolves surrounding me?
Whoa! Everything is hand-carved.
?
Diaries!
From everyone who's passed through...
Matilda...
Maybe it's the Matilda that Arne on the last island talked about...
13th September 1932
After 11 days on this island, I've finally found shelter. Before I go, I'll carve a big arrow on top of it so that everyone who comes after me can find it. I've just come from an island where I had no choice but to leave...
Bingo!

*see *Stig & Tilde: Vanisher's Island*

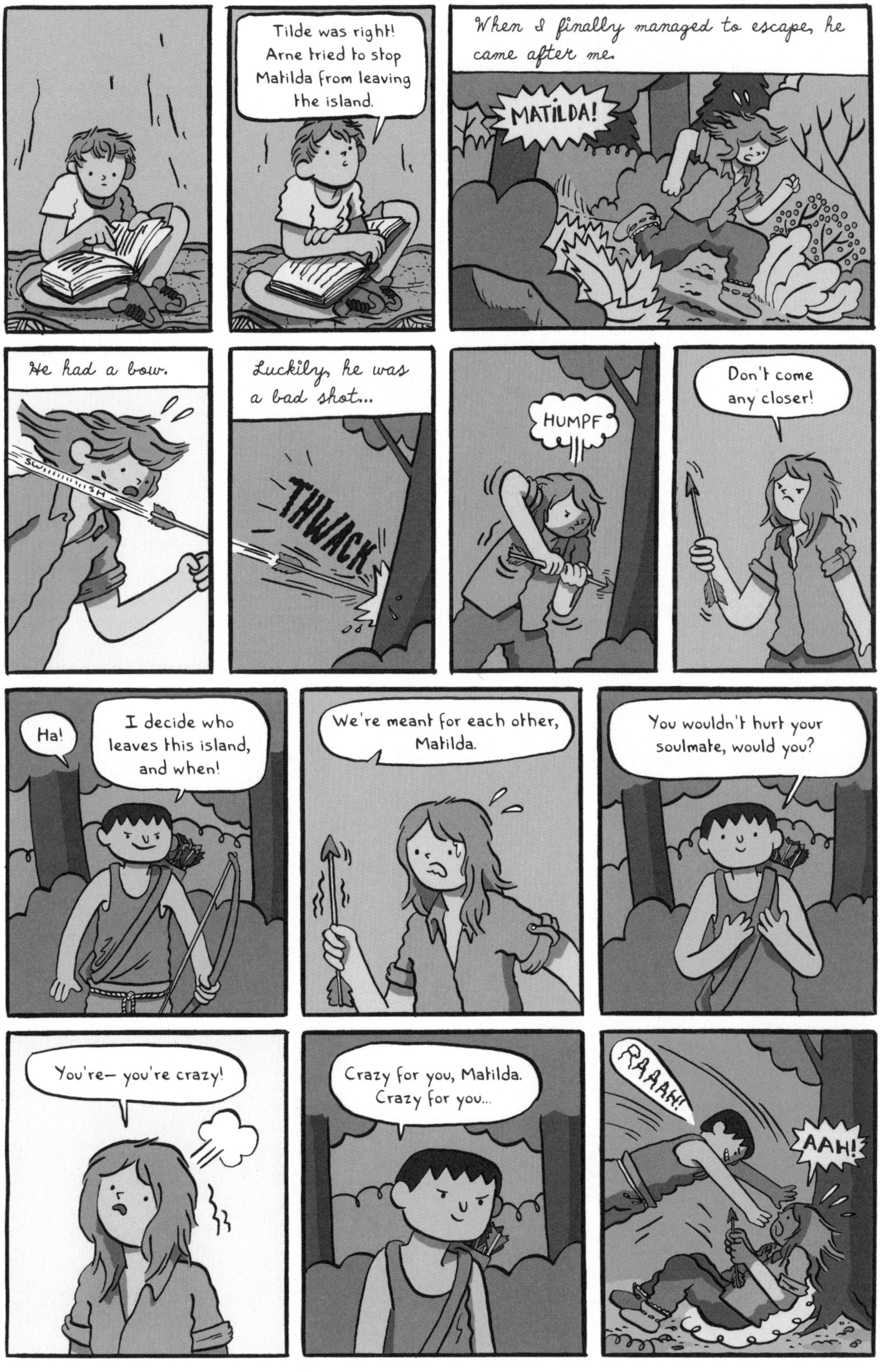
Tilde was right! Arne tried to stop Matilda from leaving the island.
When I finally managed to escape, he came after me.
MATILDA!
He had a bow.
SWIIIIIIIIISH
Luckily, he was a bad shot...
THWACK
HUMPF
Don't come any closer!
Ha!
I decide who leaves this island, and when!
We're meant for each other, Matilda.
You wouldn't hurt your soulmate, would you?
You're— you're crazy!
Crazy for you, Matilda. Crazy for you...
RAAAH!
AAH!

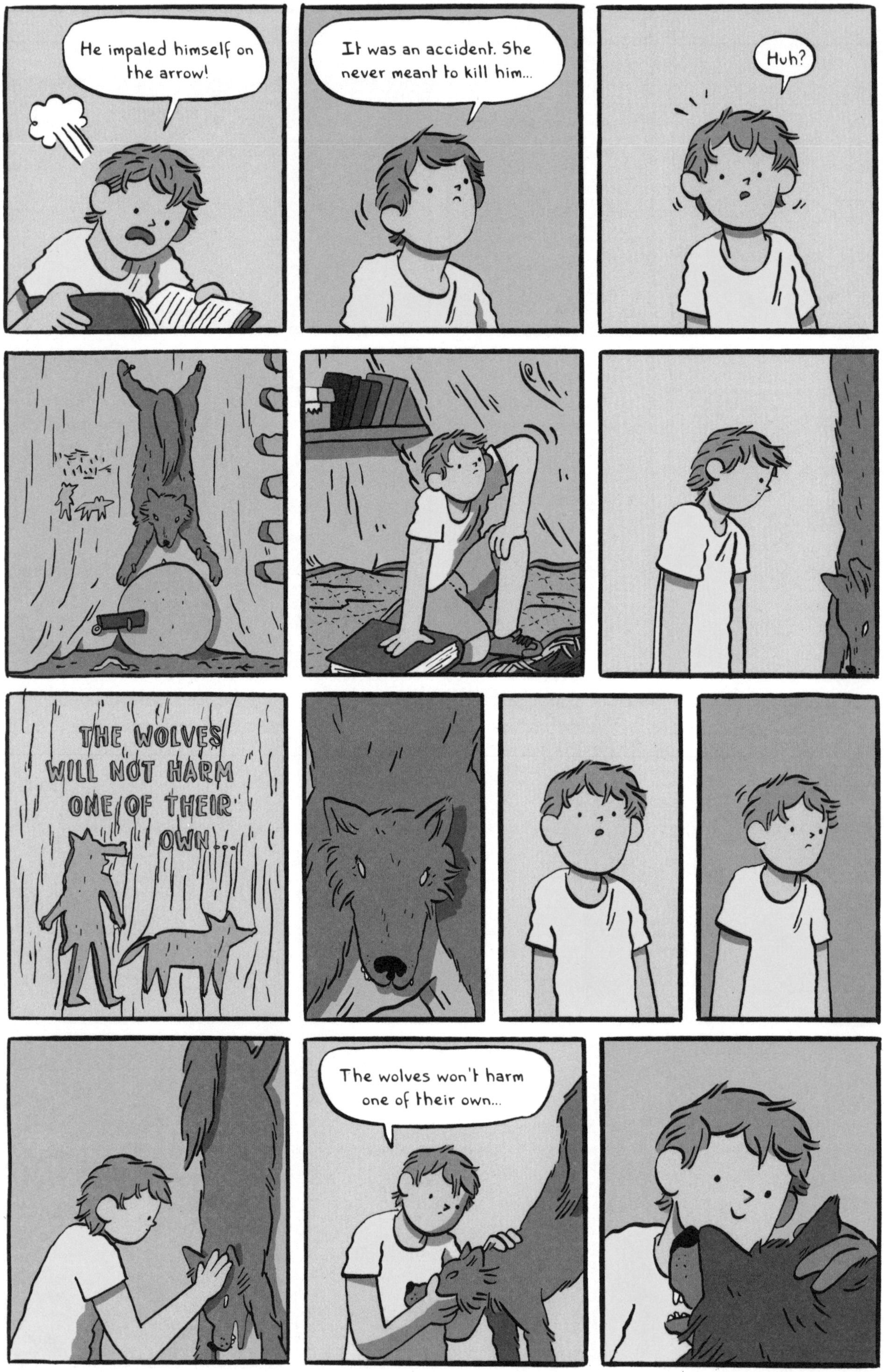
He impaled himself on the arrow!
It was an accident. She never meant to kill him...
Huh?
THE WOLVES WILL NOT HARM ONE OF THEIR OWN...
The wolves won't harm one of their own...

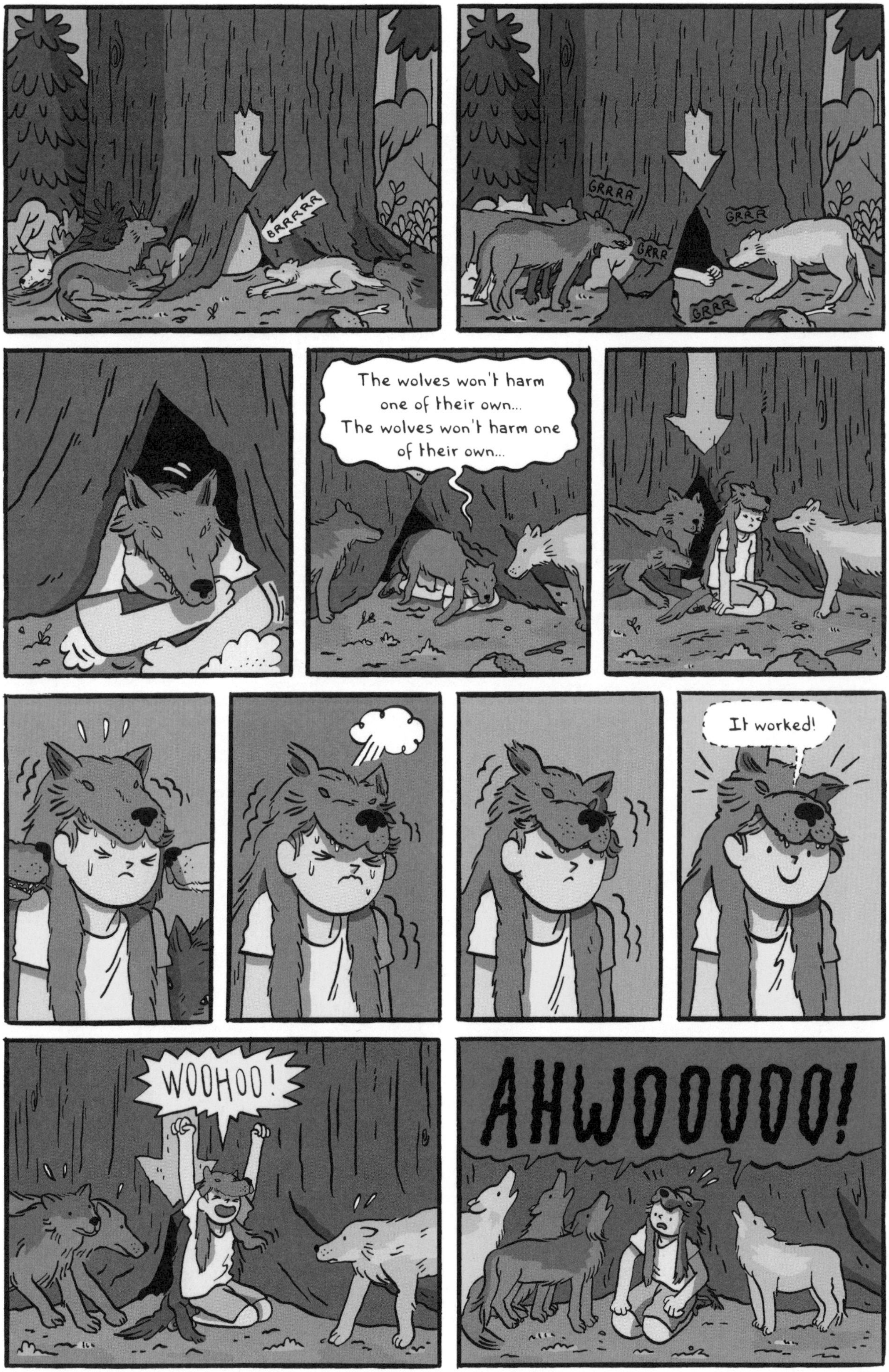
BRRRRR
GRRRR
GRRR
GRRR
GRRR
The wolves won't harm one of their own... The wolves won't harm one of their own...
It worked!
WOOHOO!
AHWOOOOO!

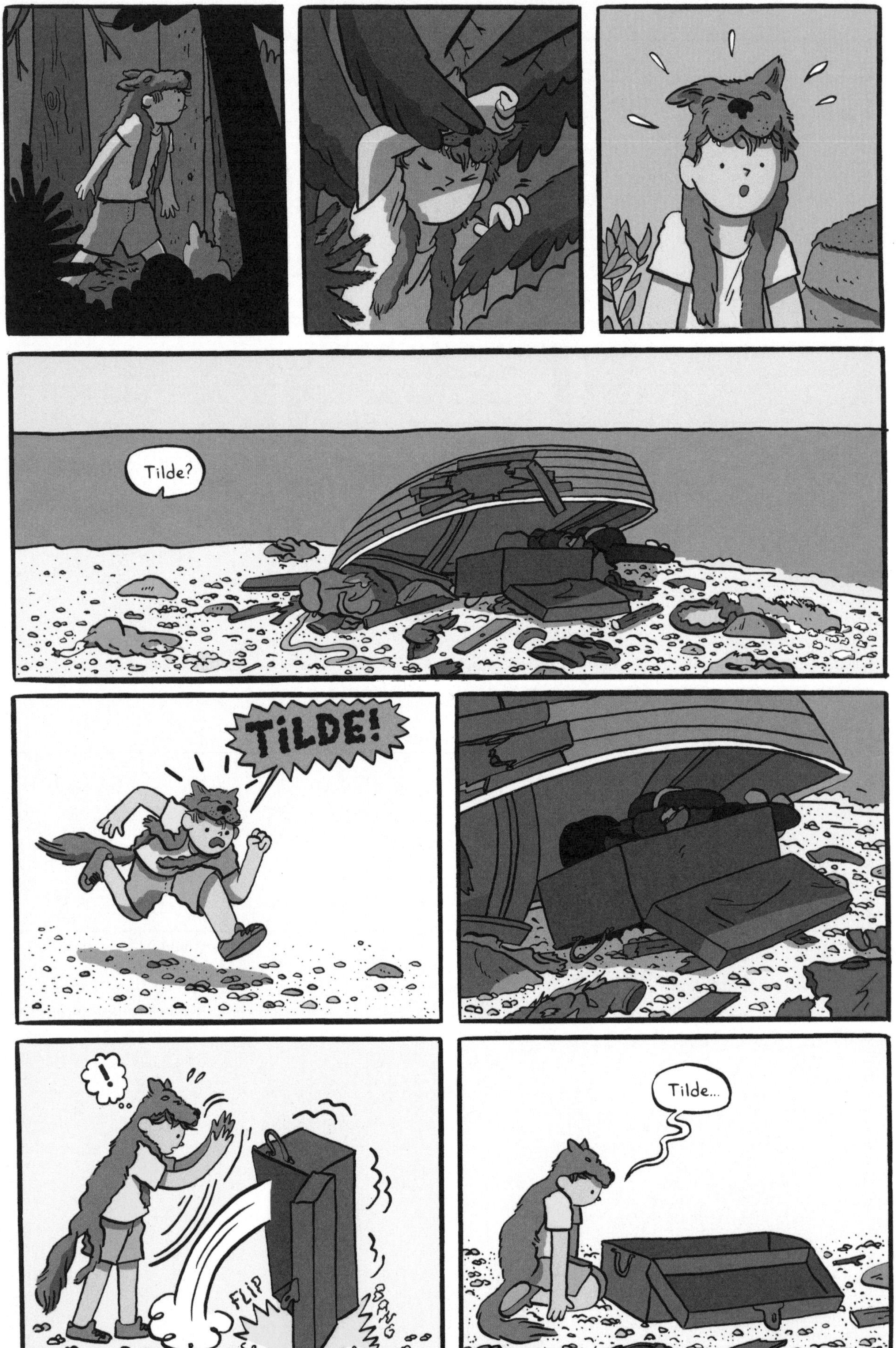
Tilde?
TILDE!
!
FLIP
BANG
Tilde...

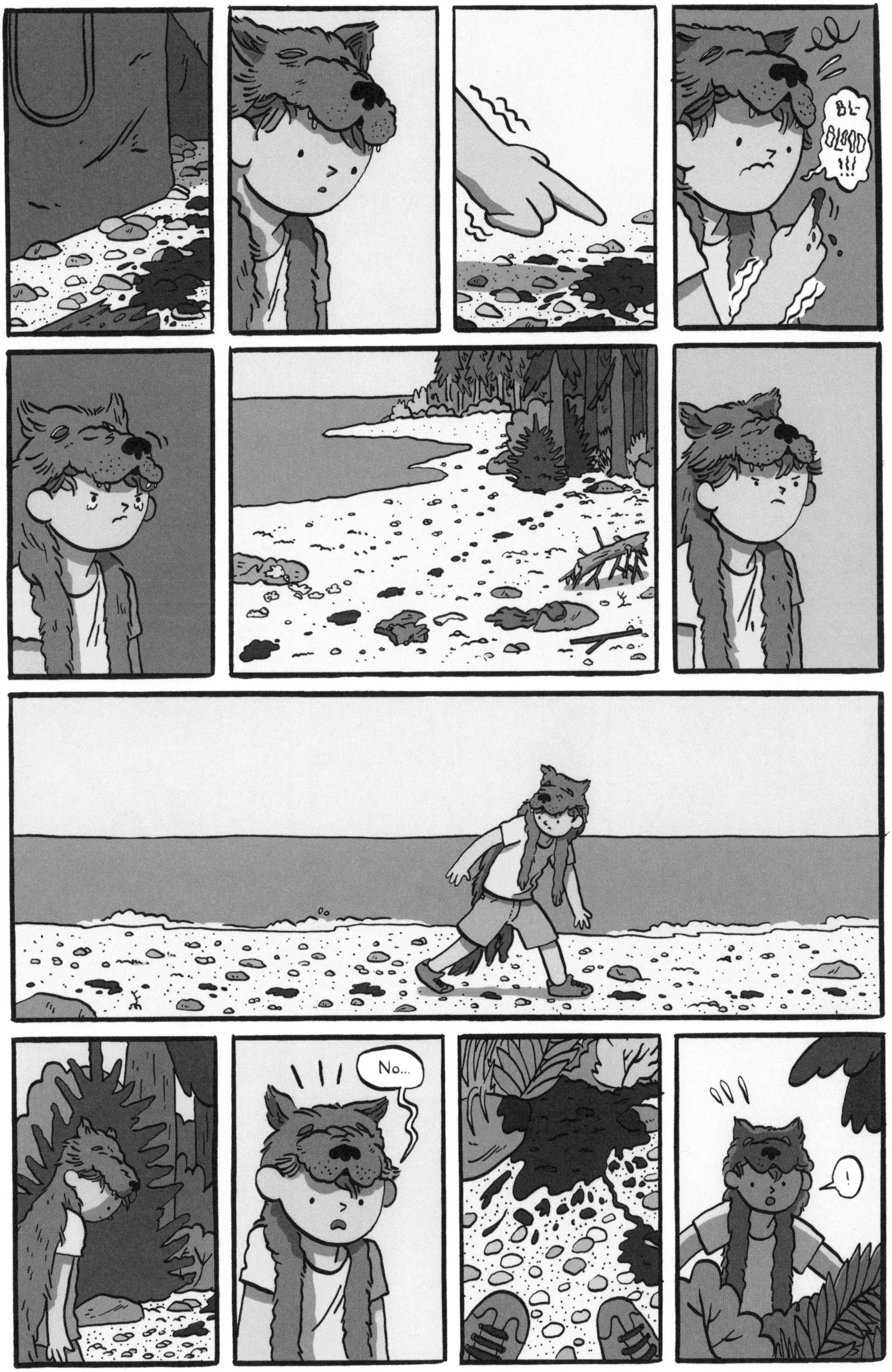
BL-
BLOOD
!!!
No...
!

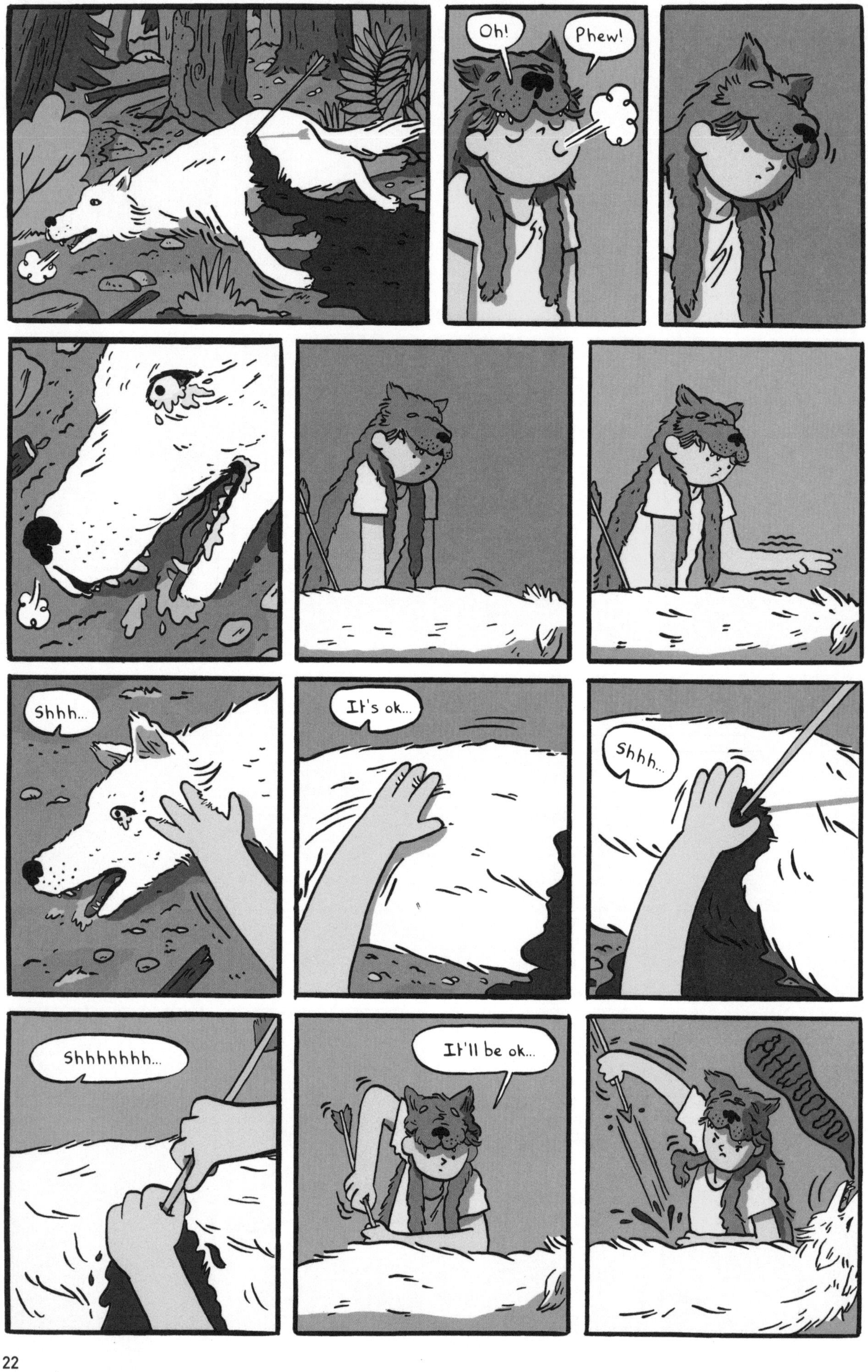
Oh!
Phew!
Shhh...
It's ok...
Shhh...
Shhhhhhh...
It'll be ok...
AHWOOOOO

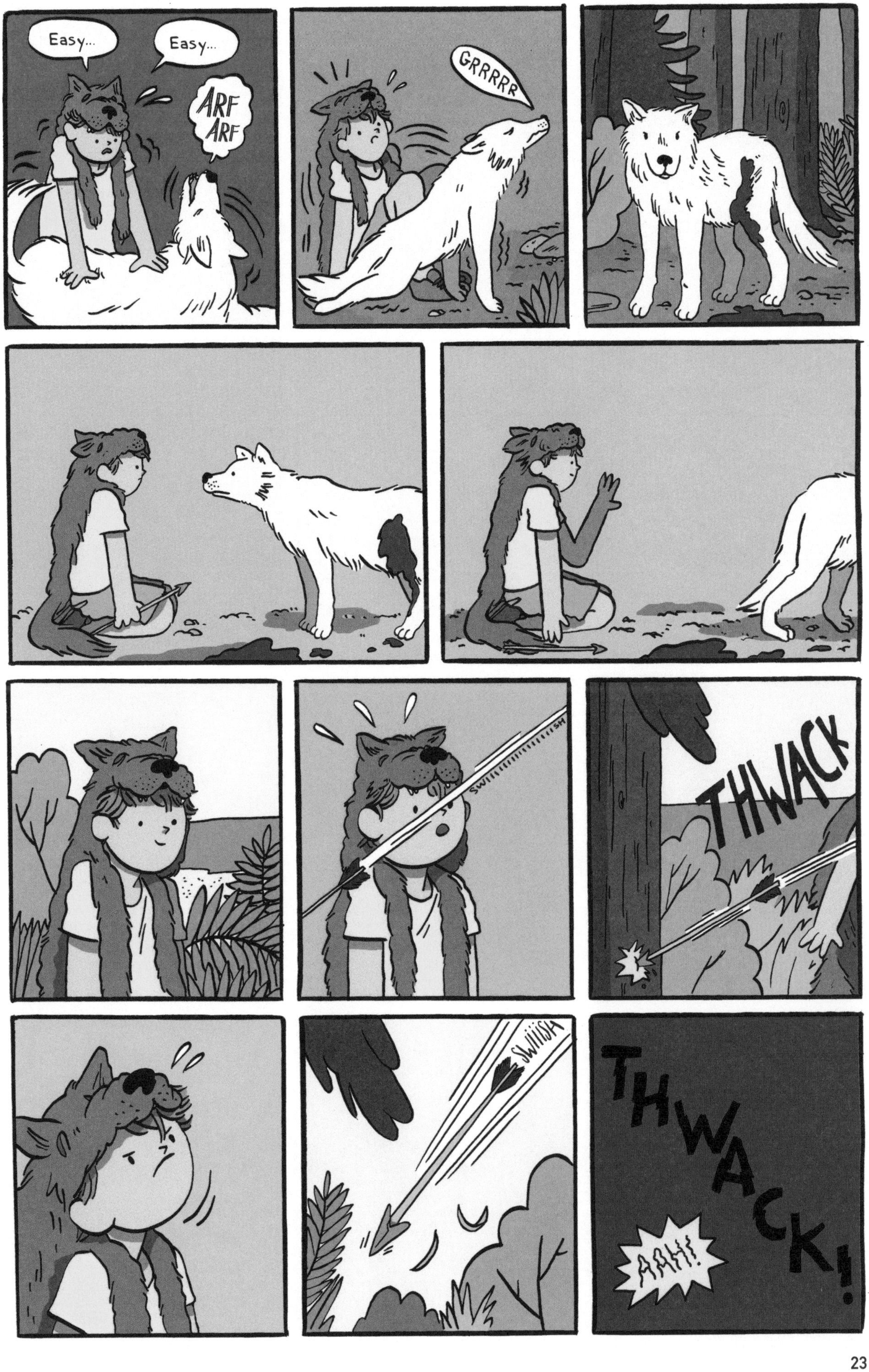
Easy...
Easy...
ARF ARF
GRRRRR
SWIIIIIIIIIIIISH
THWACK
SWIIISH
THWACK!
ARH!

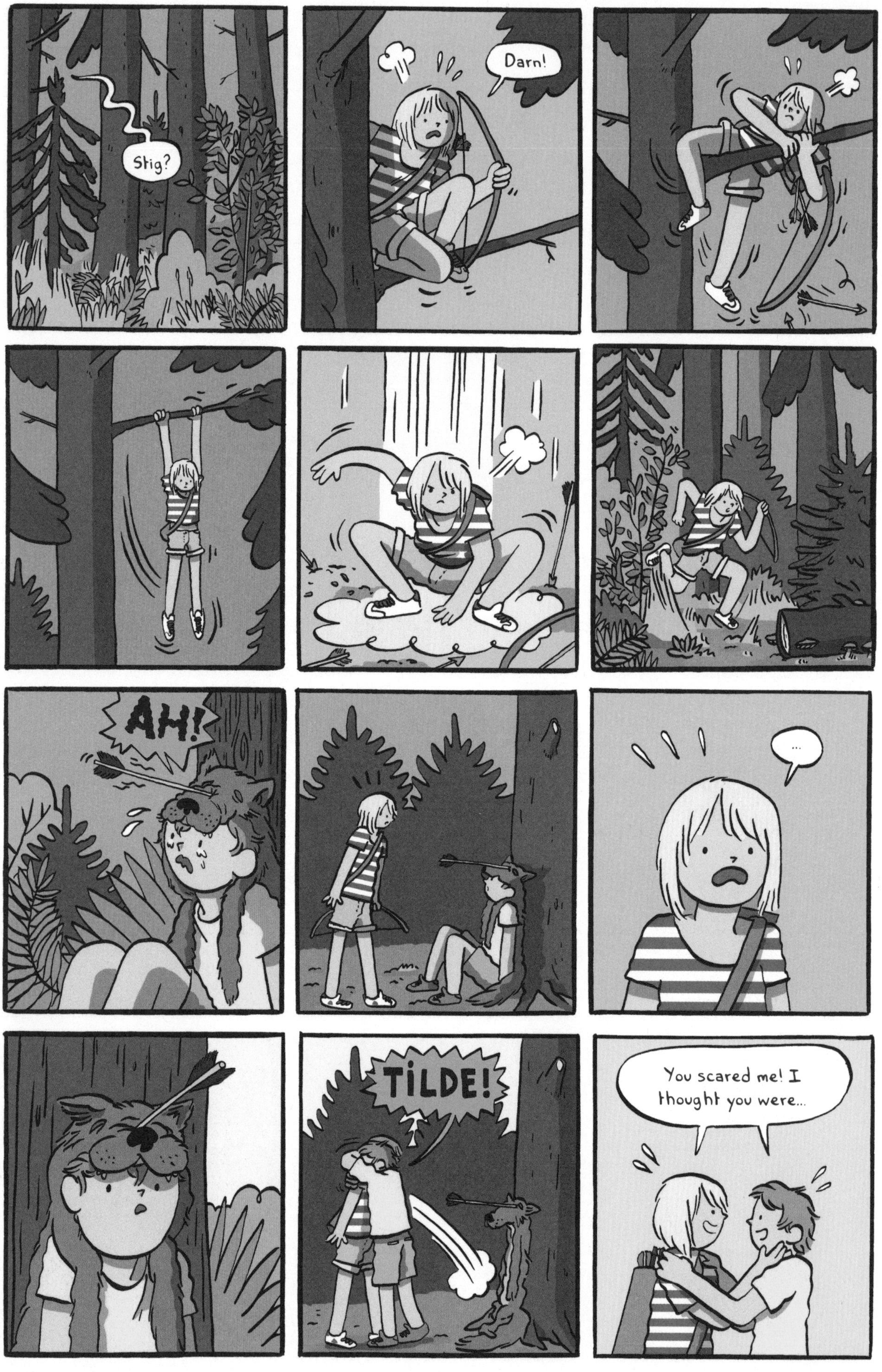
Stig?
Darn!
AH!
...
TILDE!
You scared me! I thought you were...

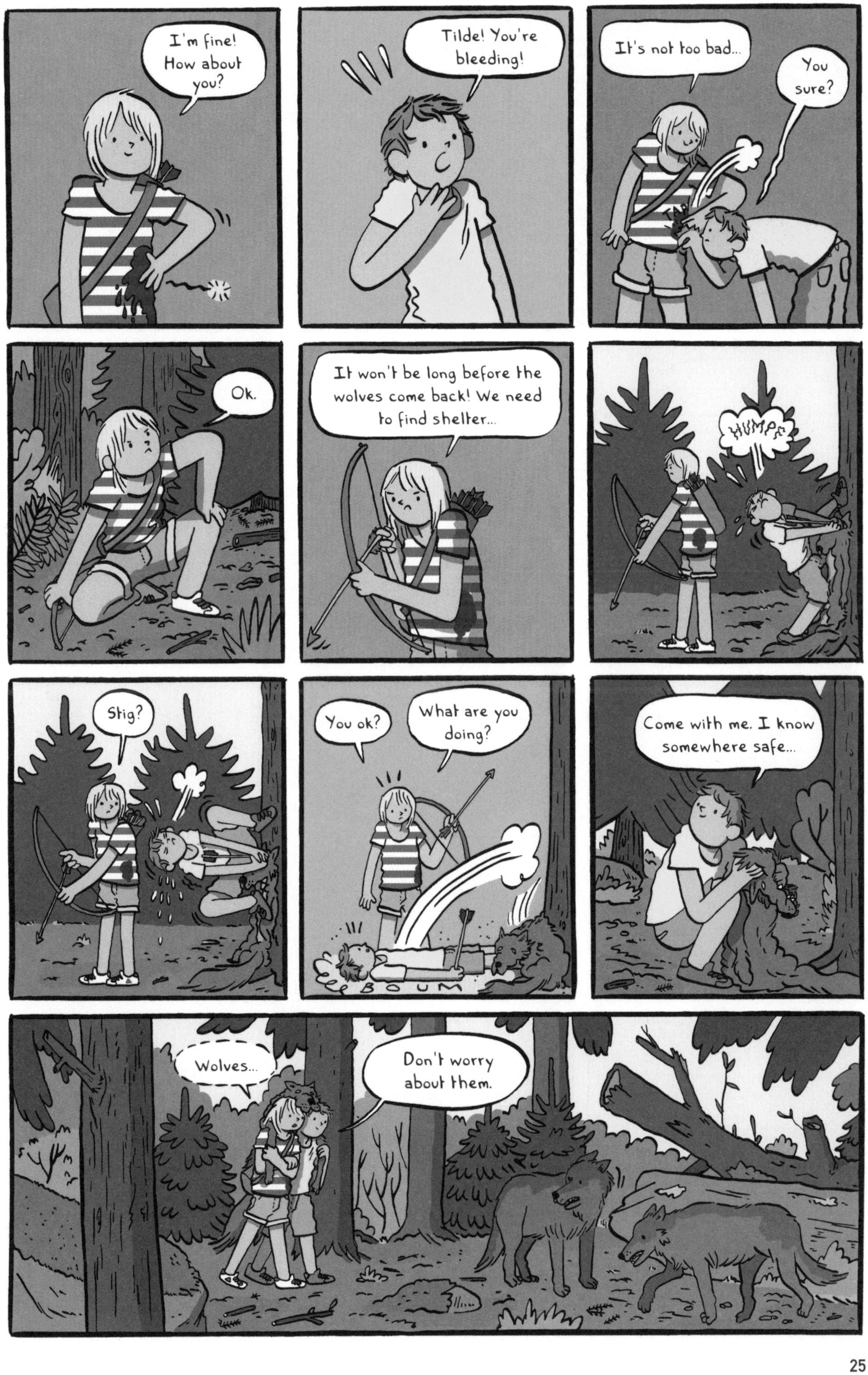
I'm fine! How about you?
Tilde! You're bleeding!
It's not too bad...
You sure?
Ok.
It won't be long before the wolves come back! We need to find shelter...
HUMPF
Stig?
You ok?
What are you doing?
BOUM
Come with me. I know somewhere safe...
Wolves...
Don't worry about them.

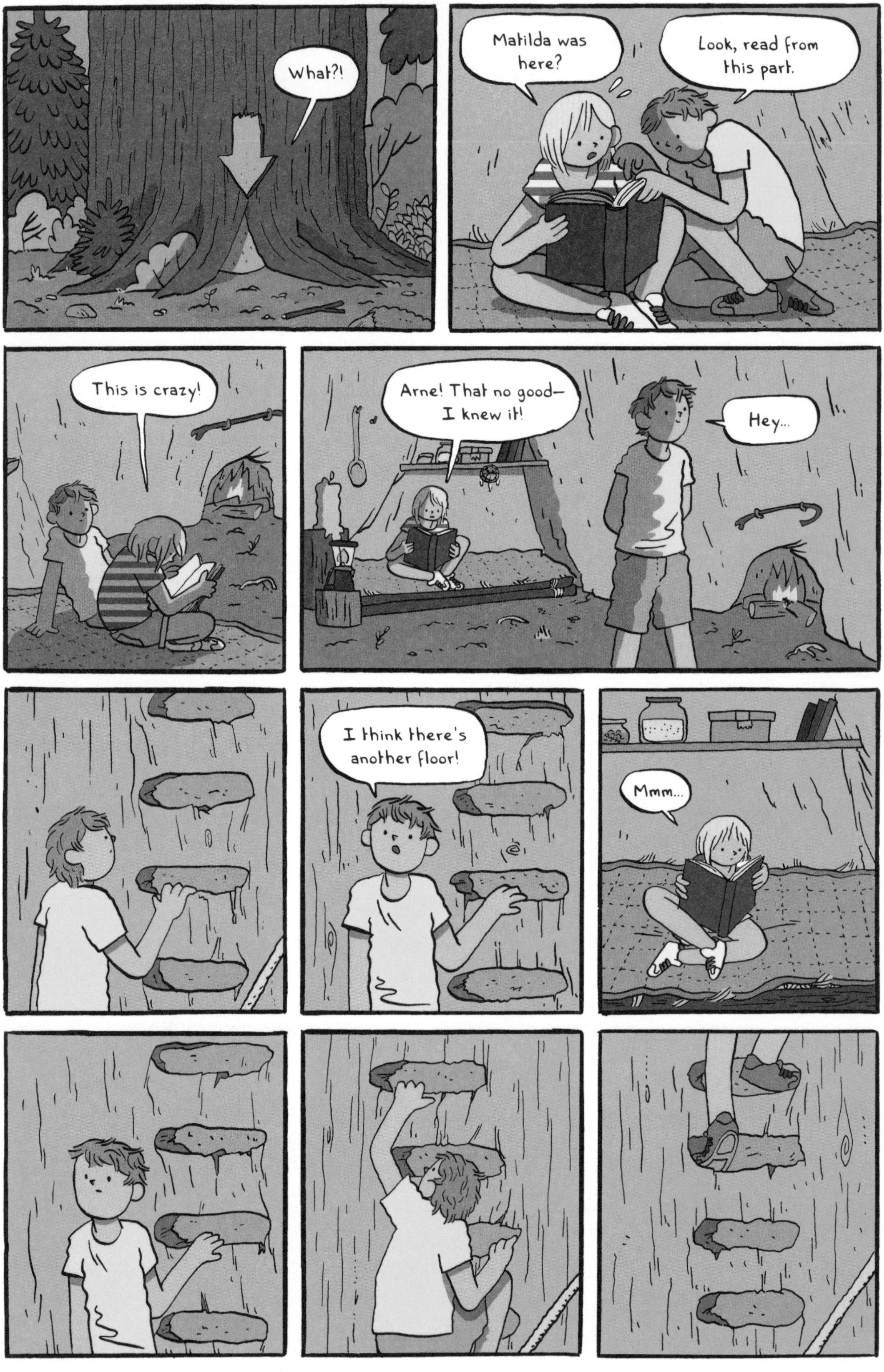
What?!
Matilda was here?
Look, read from this part.
This is crazy!
Arne! That no good— I knew it!
Hey...
I think there's another floor!
Mmm...

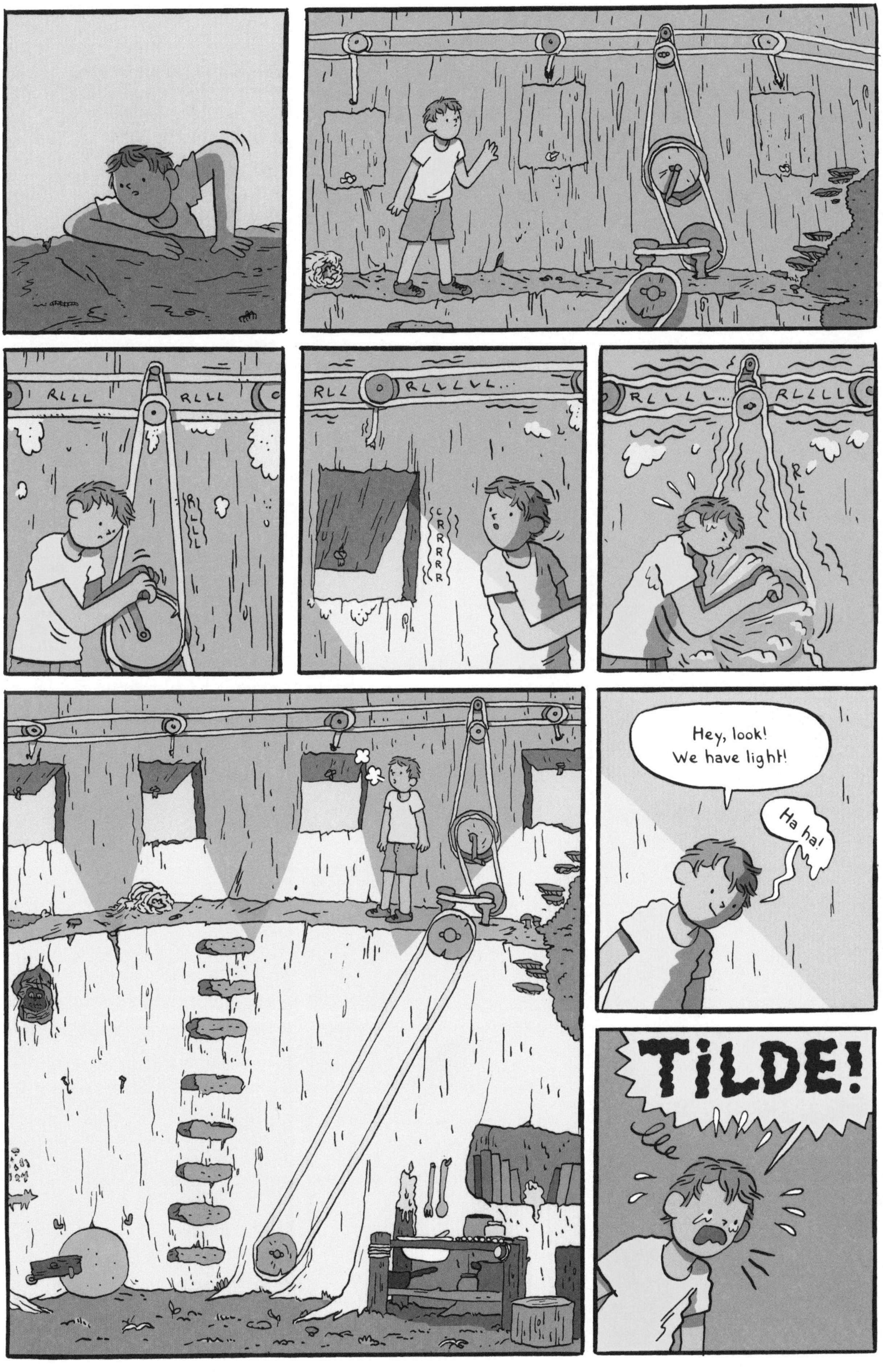
RLLL
RLLL
RLLL
RLL
RLLLLL...
RRRRR
RLLLL...
RLLLL
RLLL
Hey, look! We have light!
Ha ha!
TILDE!

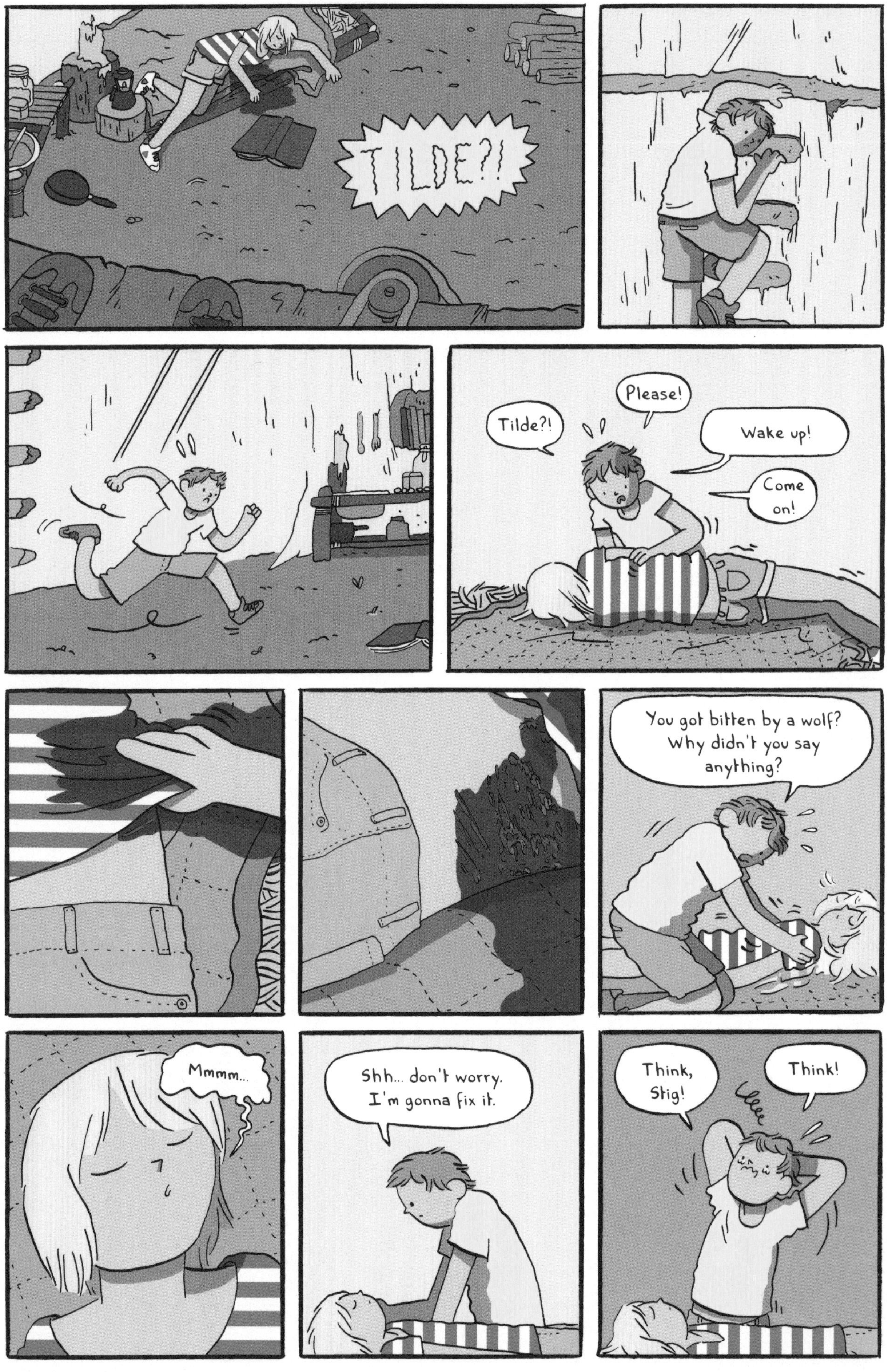

TILDE?!
Tilde?!
Please!
Wake up!
Come on!
You got bitten by a wolf? Why didn't you say anything?
Mmmm...
Shh... don't worry. I'm gonna fix it.
Think, Stig!
Think!

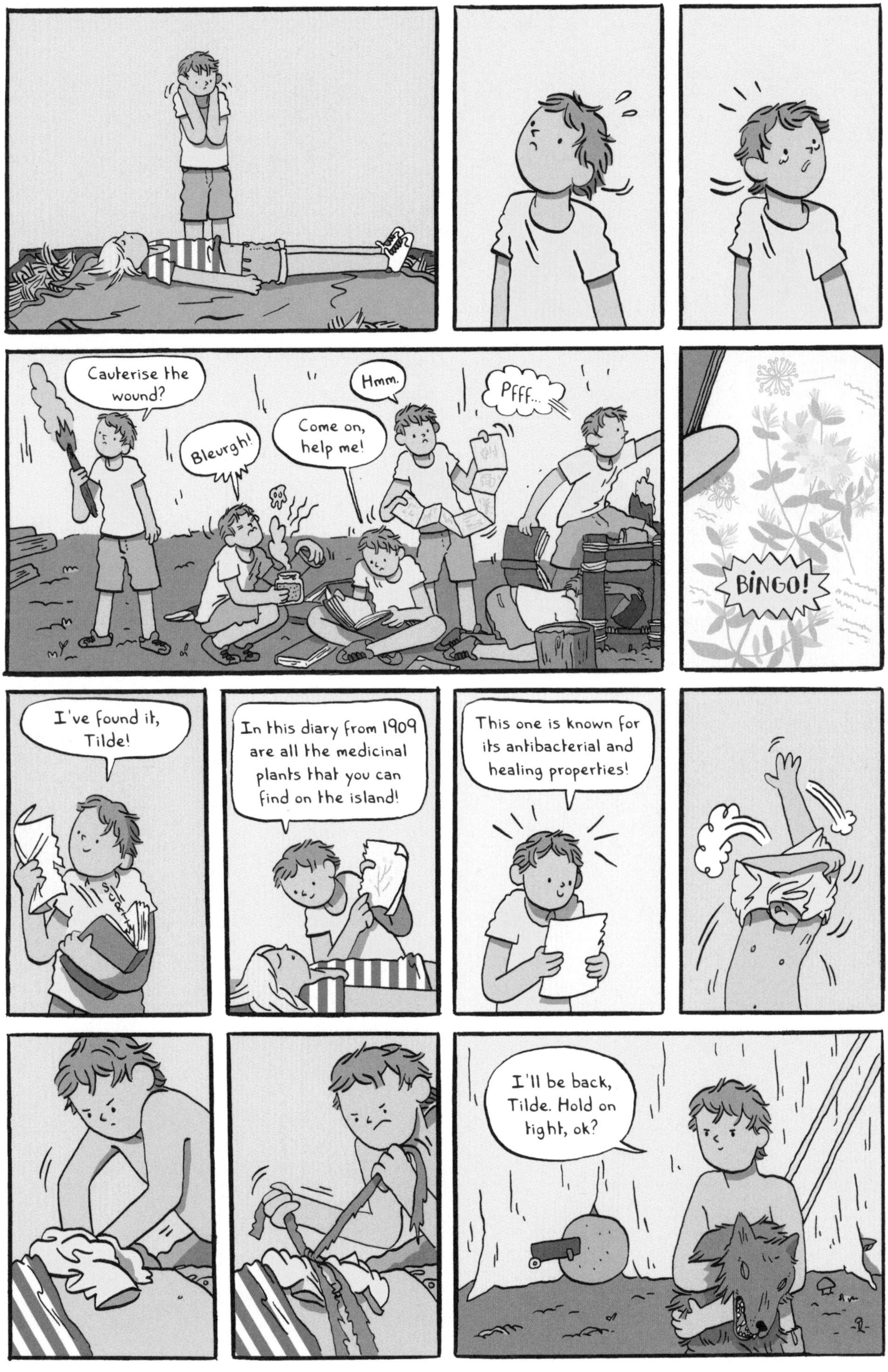

Cauterise the wound?
Bleurgh!
Come on, help me!
Hmm.
Pfff...
BINGO!
I've found it, Tilde!
In this diary from 1909 are all the medicinal plants that you can find on the island!
This one is known for its antibacterial and healing properties!
I'll be back, Tilde. Hold on tight, ok?

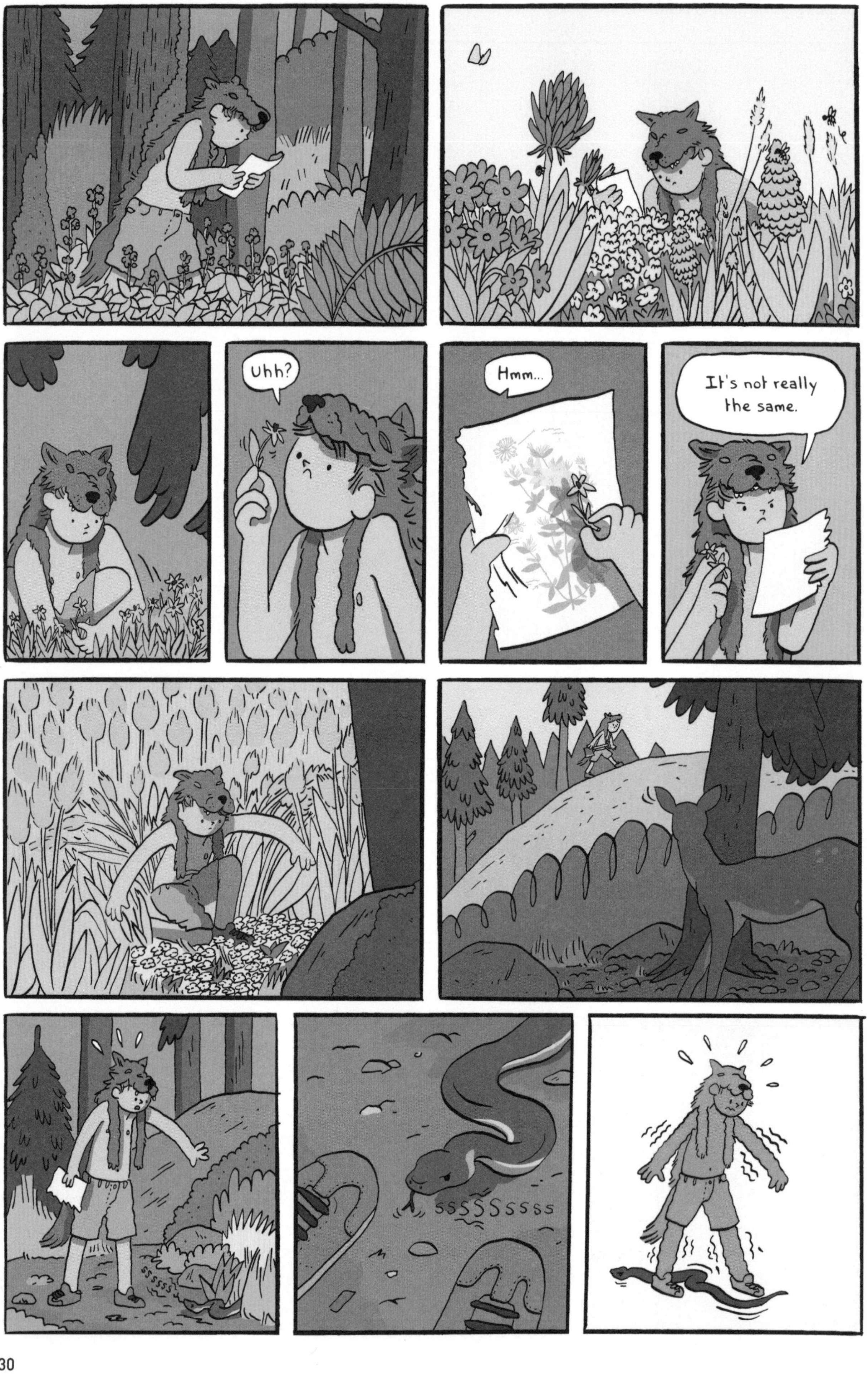
Uhh?
Hmm...
It's not really the same.
SSSSSS
SSSSSSSSS

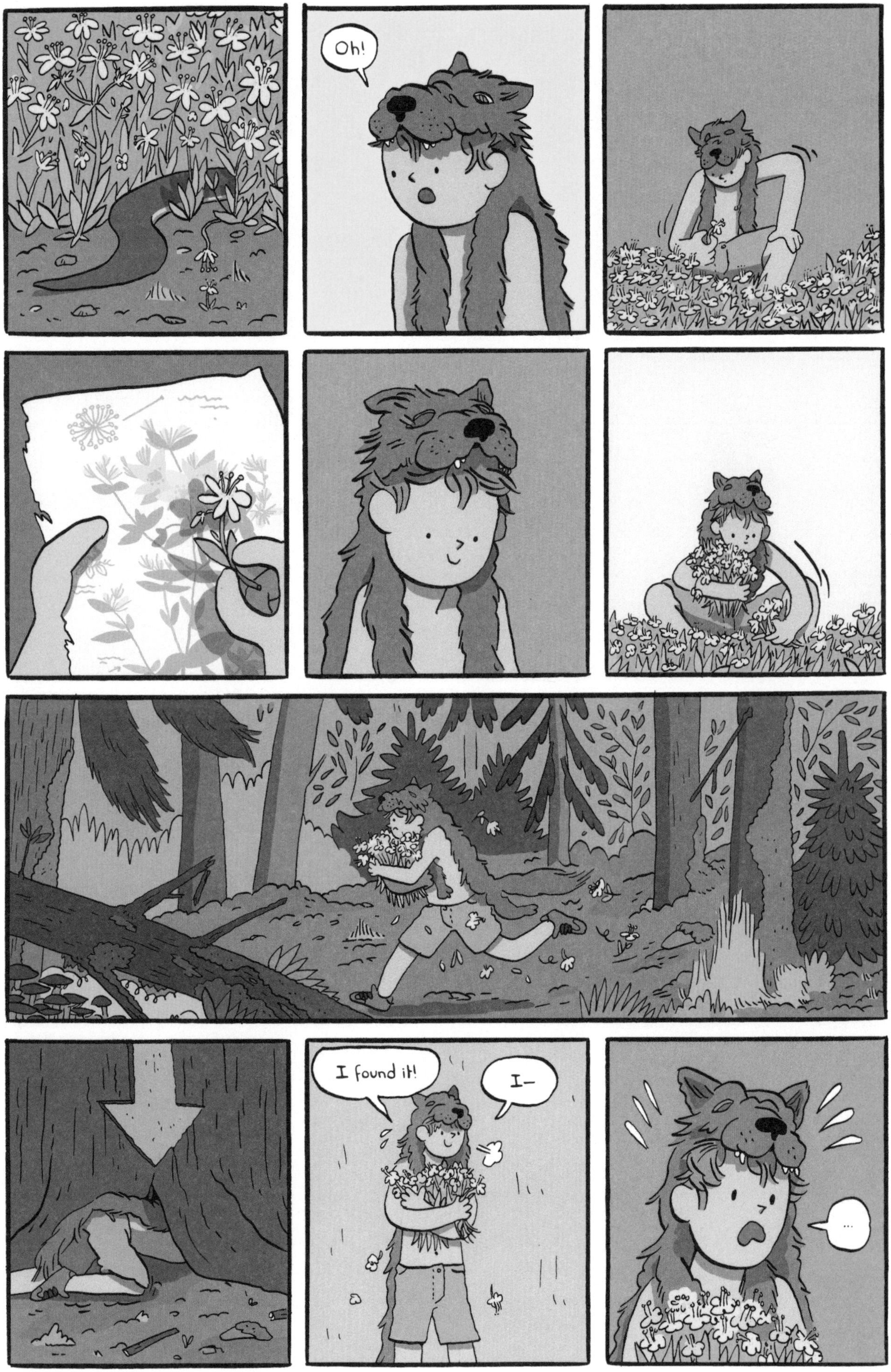
Oh!
I found it!
I–
...

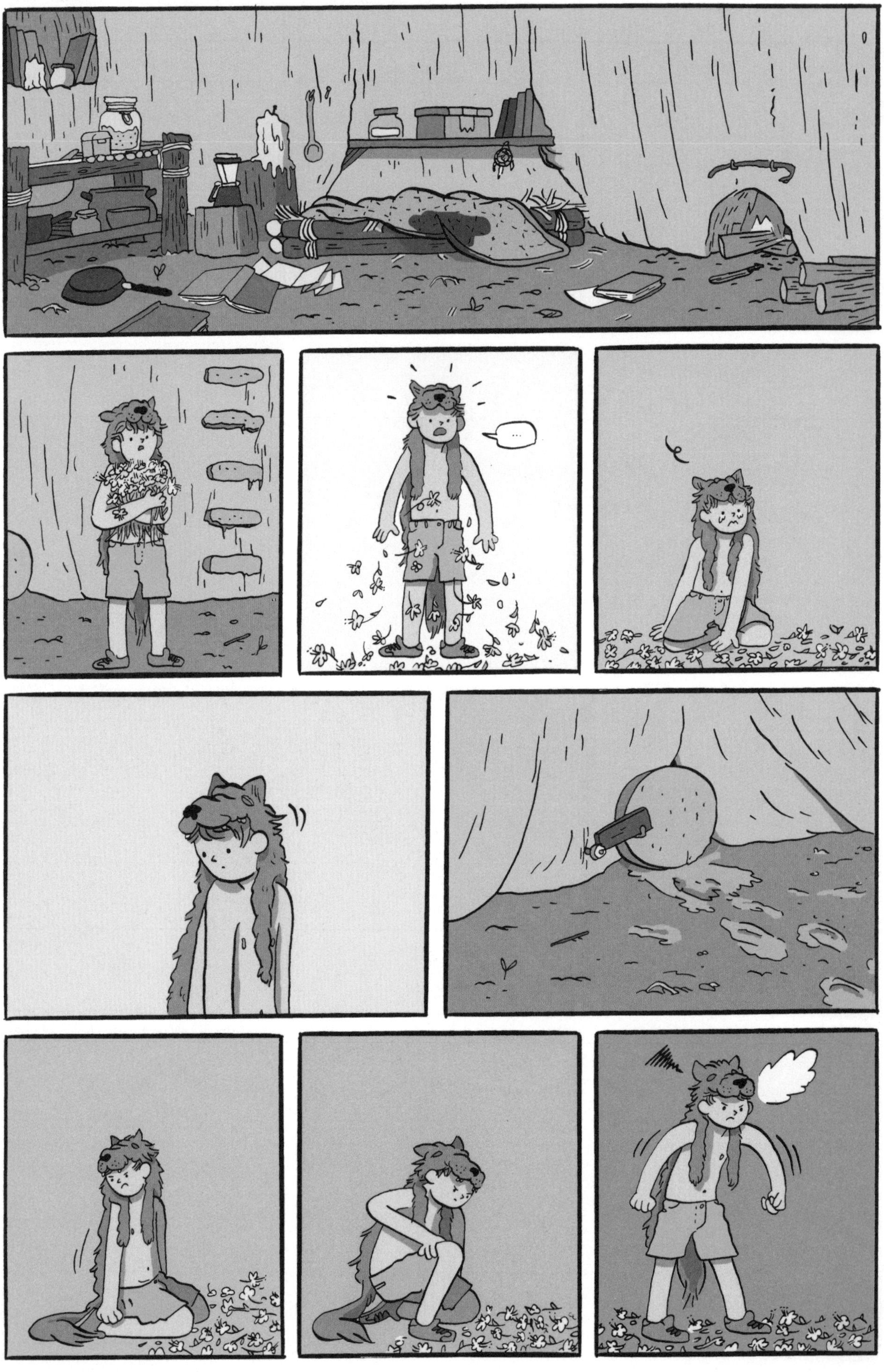
...

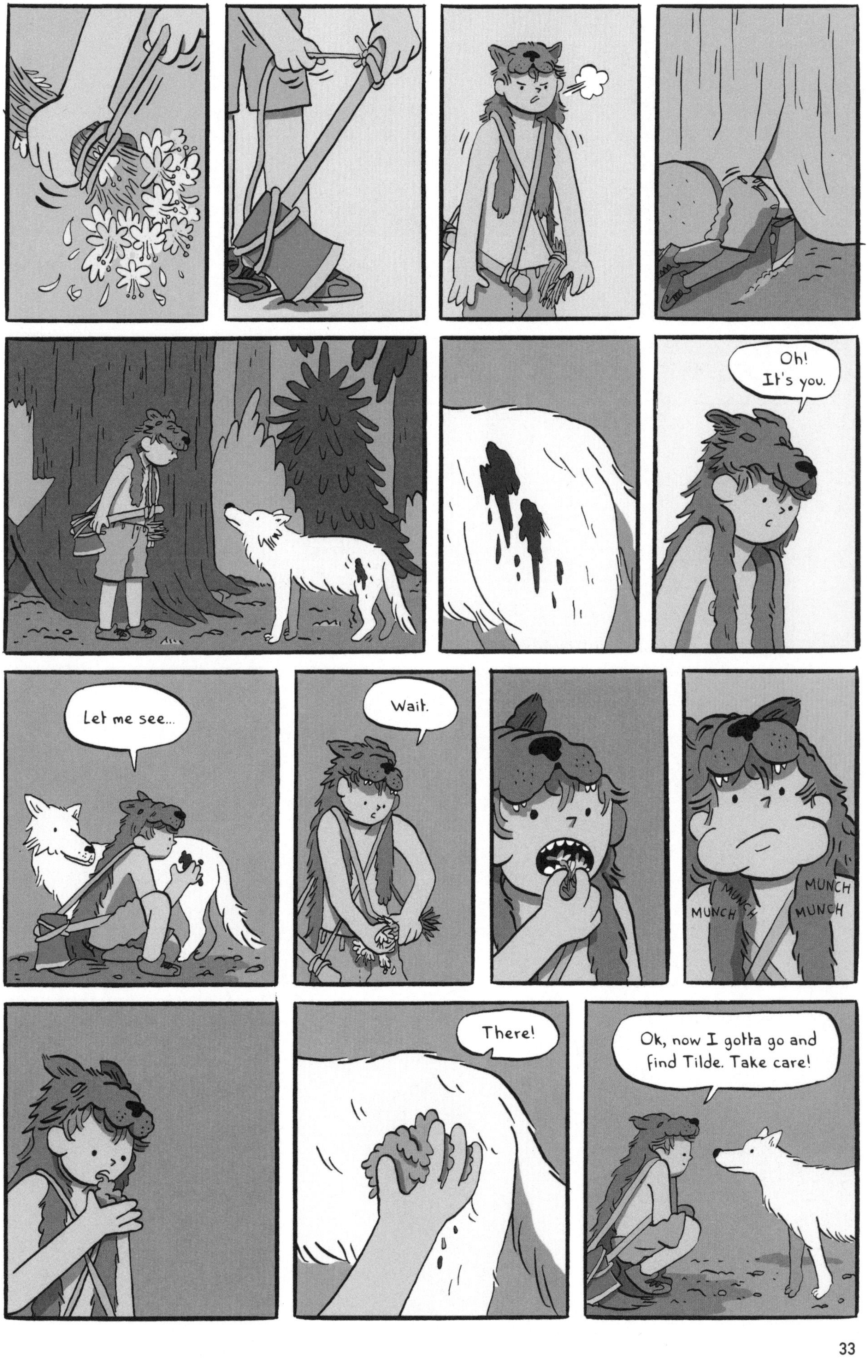

Oh! It's you.
Let me see...
Wait.
MUNCH
MUNCH
MUNCH
MUNCH
There!
Ok, now I gotta go and find Tilde. Take care!

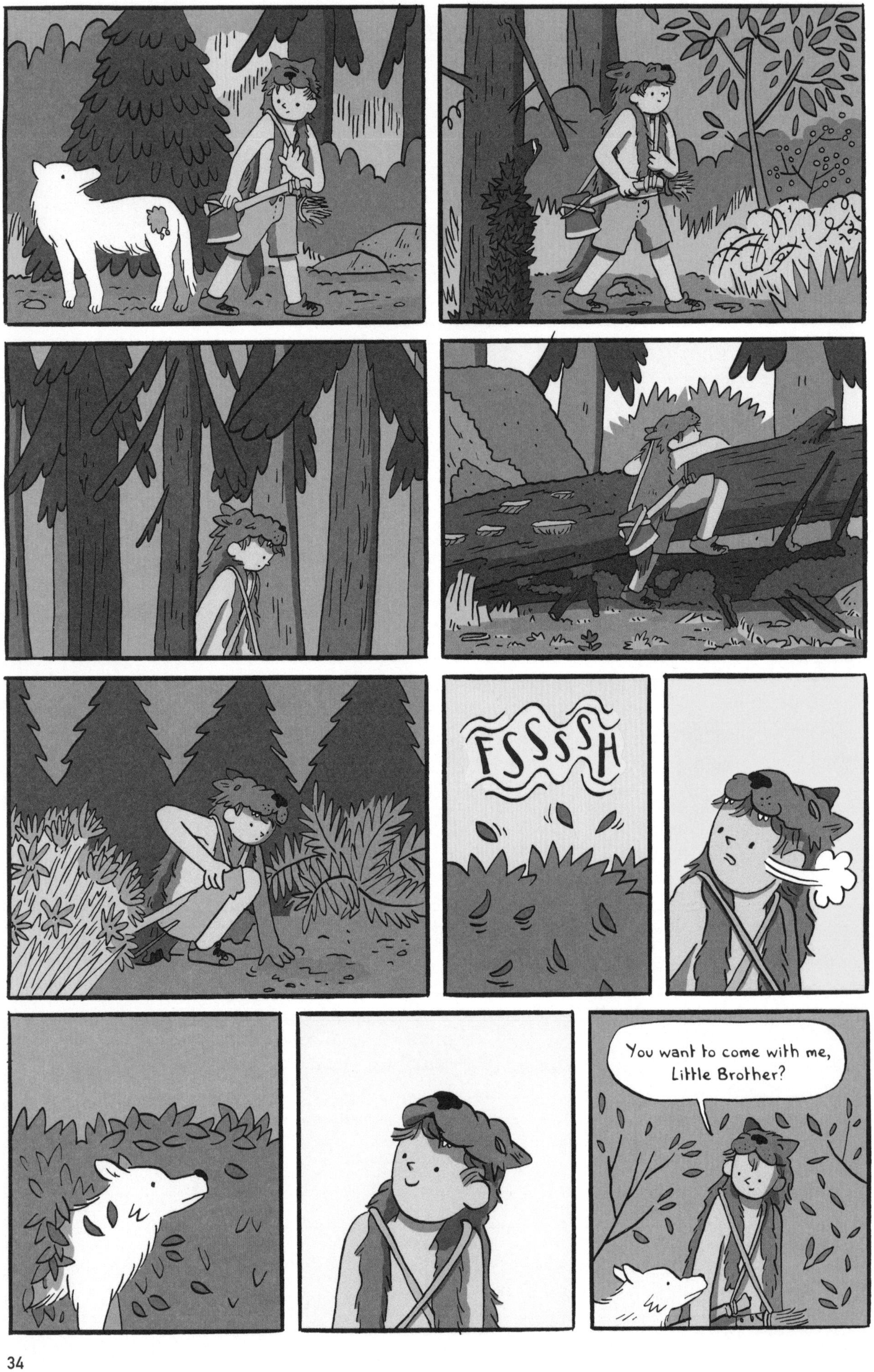
FSSSSH
You want to come with me, Little Brother?

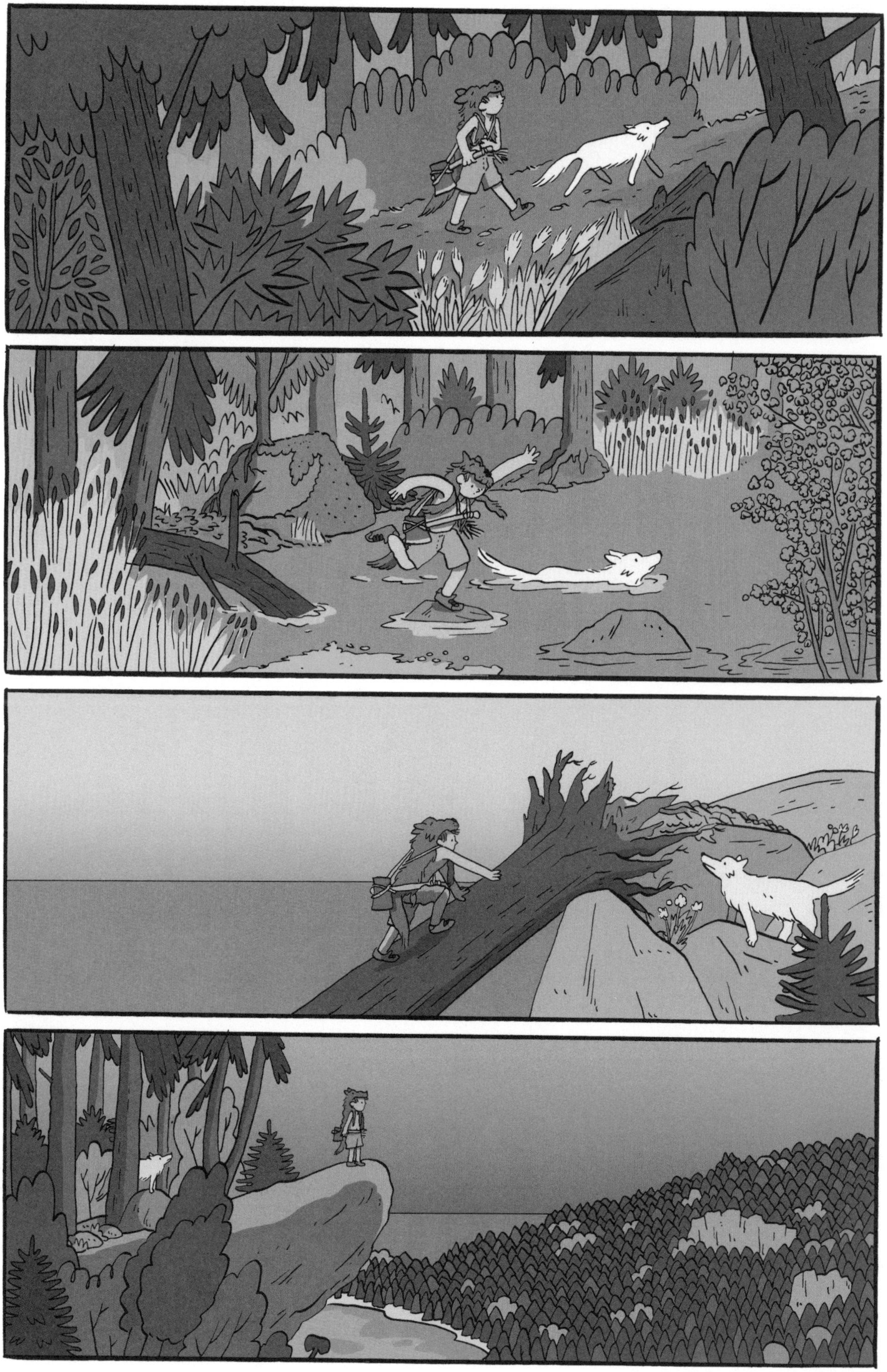

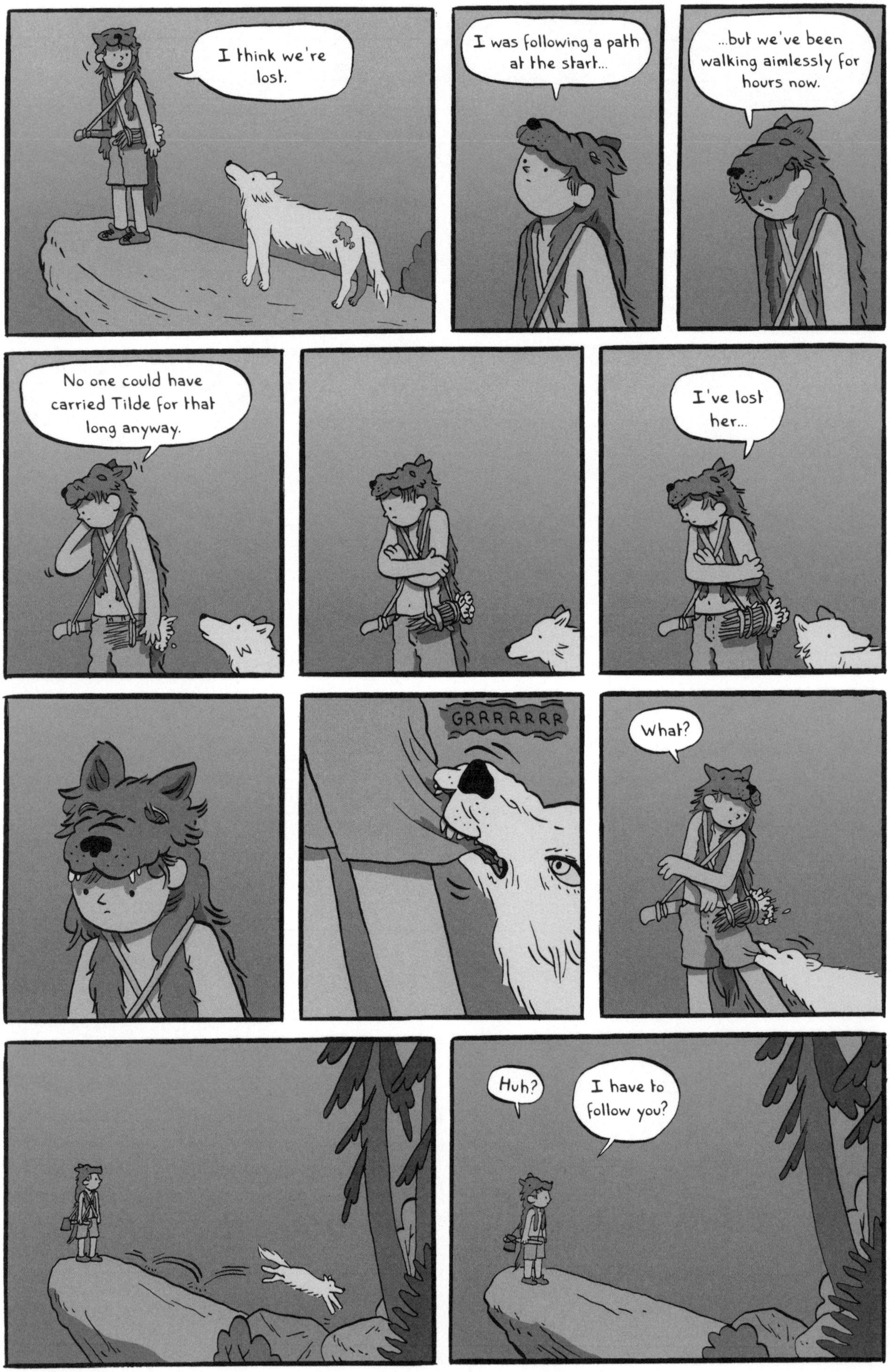

I think we're lost.
I was following a path at the start...
...but we've been walking aimlessly for hours now.
No one could have carried Tilde for that long anyway.
I've lost her...
GRRRRRRR
What?
Huh?
I have to follow you?

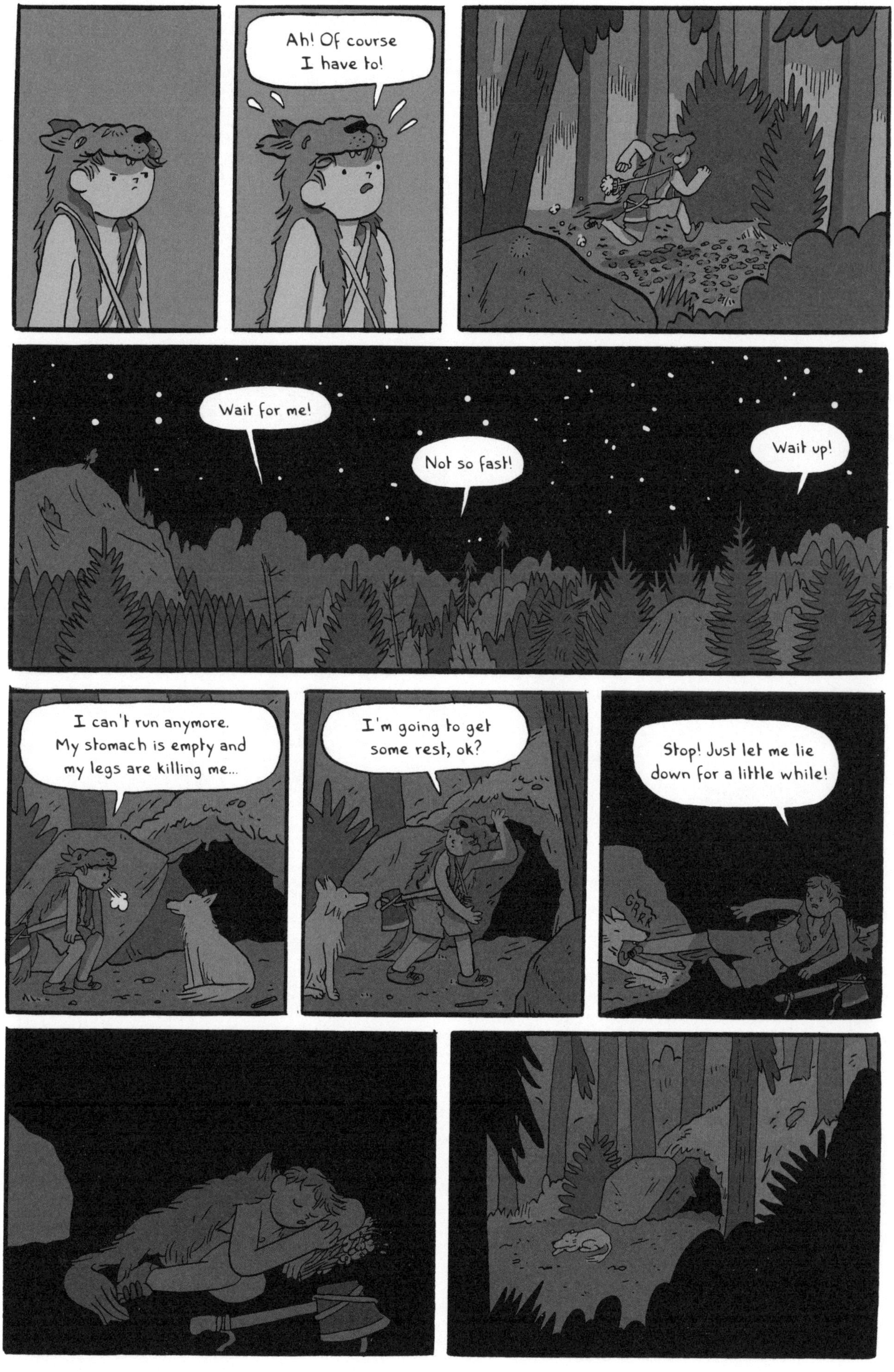
Ah! Of course I have to!
Wait for me!
Not so fast!
Wait up!
I can't run anymore. My stomach is empty and my legs are killing me...
I'm going to get some rest, ok?
Stop! Just let me lie down for a little while!
GRRR

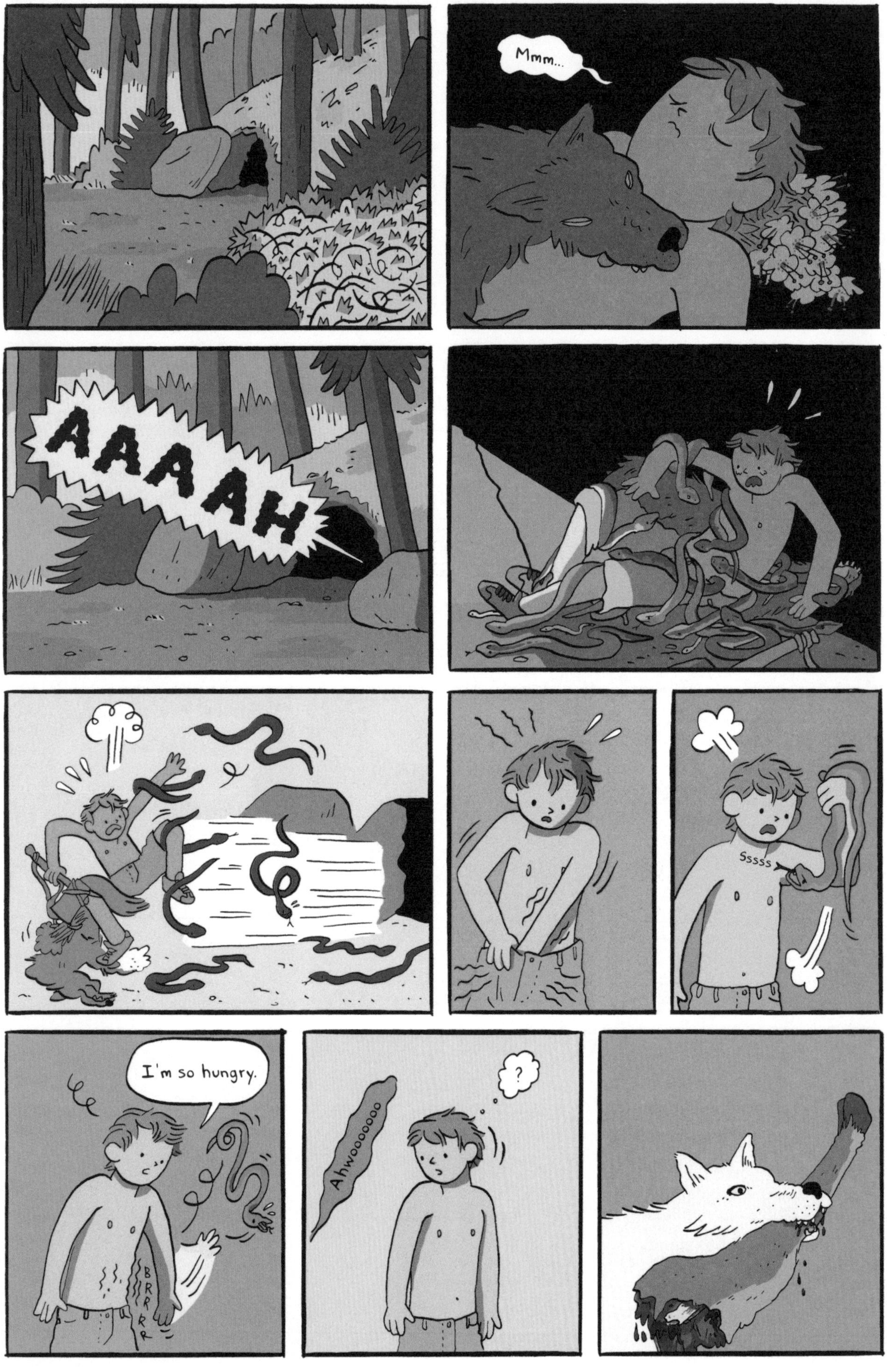

Mmm...
AAAAH
Sssss
I'm so hungry.
BRRRR
?
Ahwoooooooo

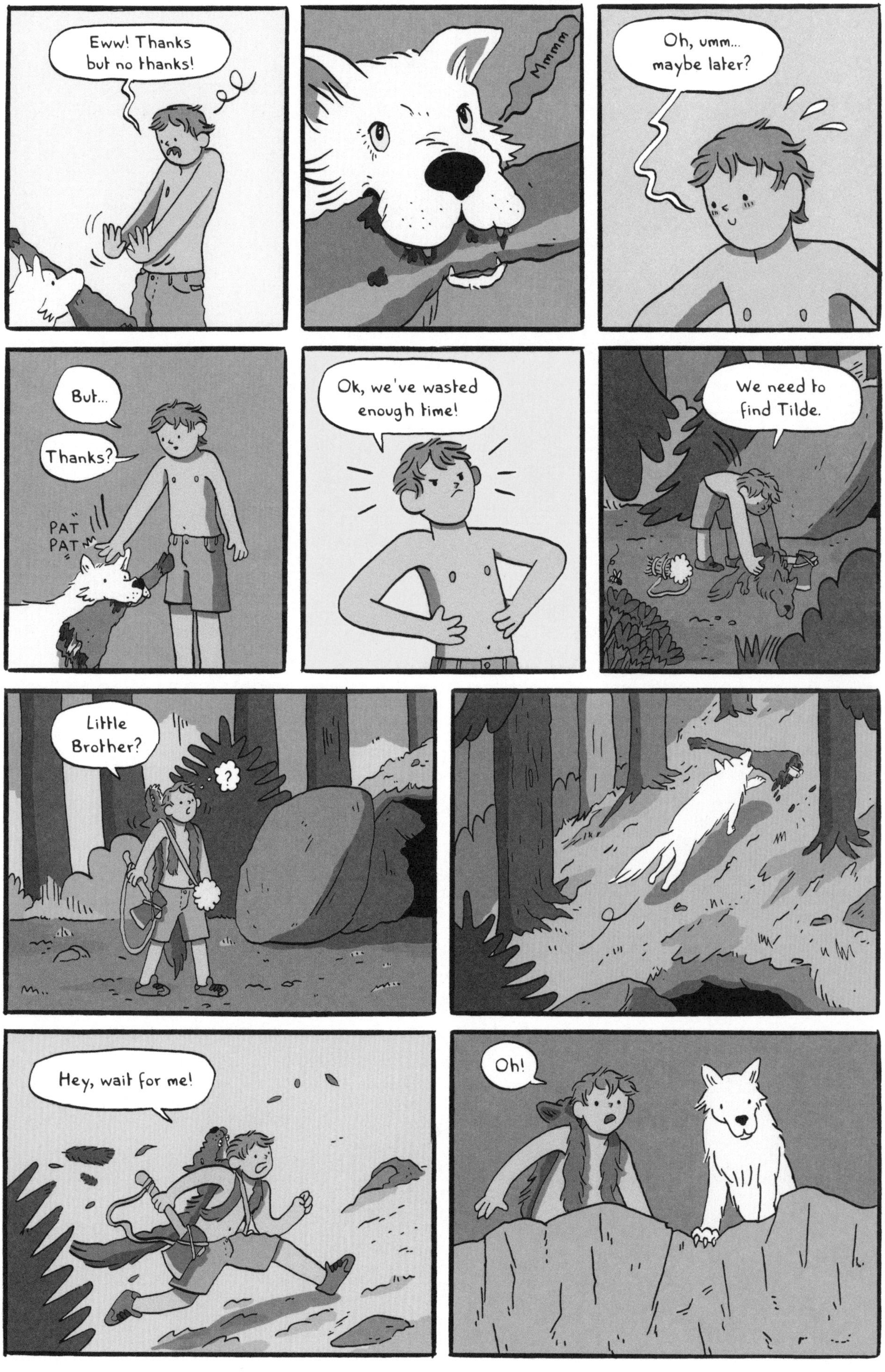
Eww! Thanks but no thanks!
Mmmm
Oh, umm... maybe later?
But...
Thanks?
PAT PAT
Ok, we've wasted enough time!
We need to find Tilde.
Little Brother?
?
Hey, wait for me!
Oh!

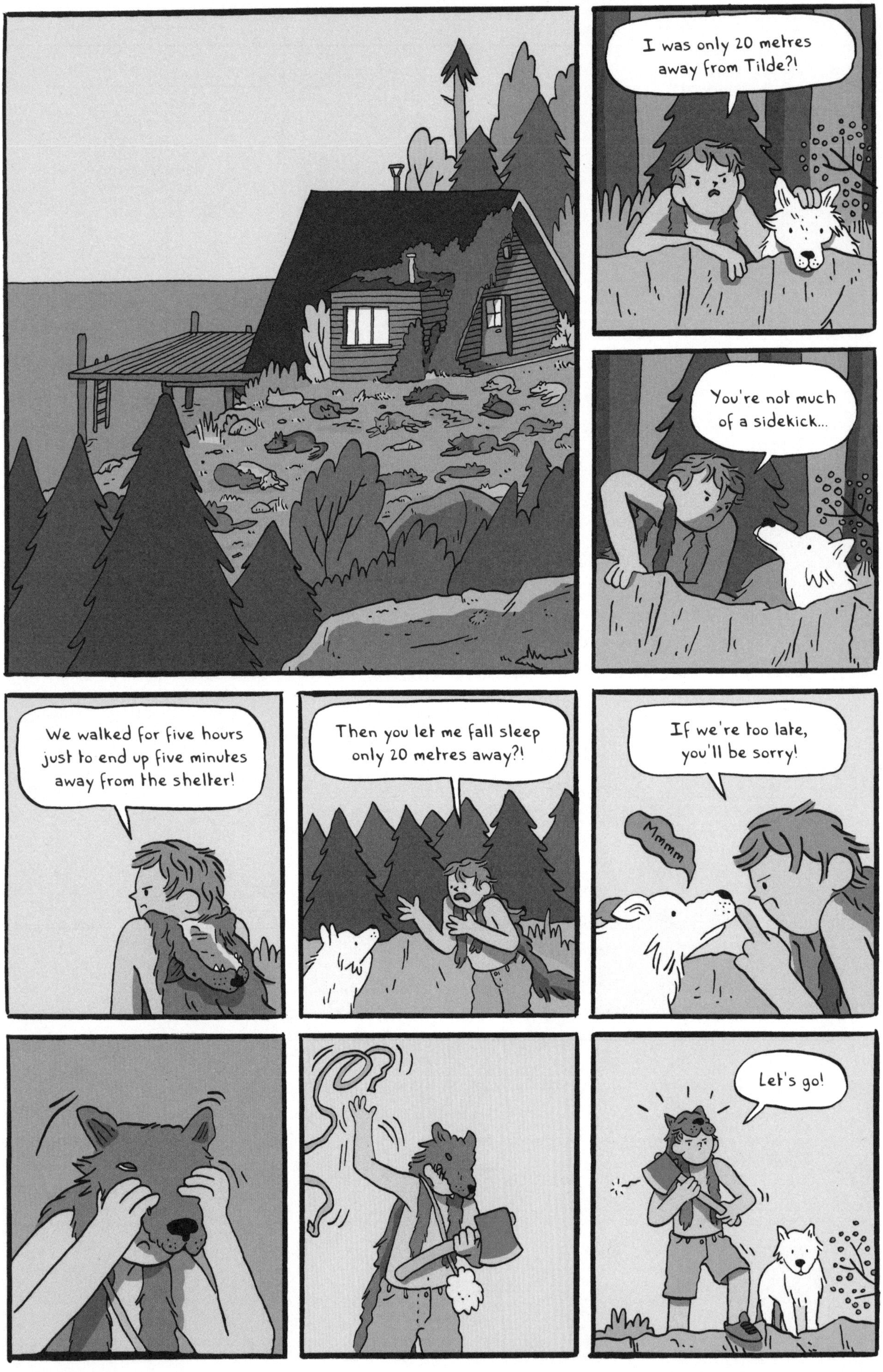

I was only 20 metres away from Tilde?!
You're not much of a sidekick...
We walked for five hours just to end up five minutes away from the shelter!
Then you let me fall sleep only 20 metres away?!
If we're too late, you'll be sorry!
Mmmm
Let's go!

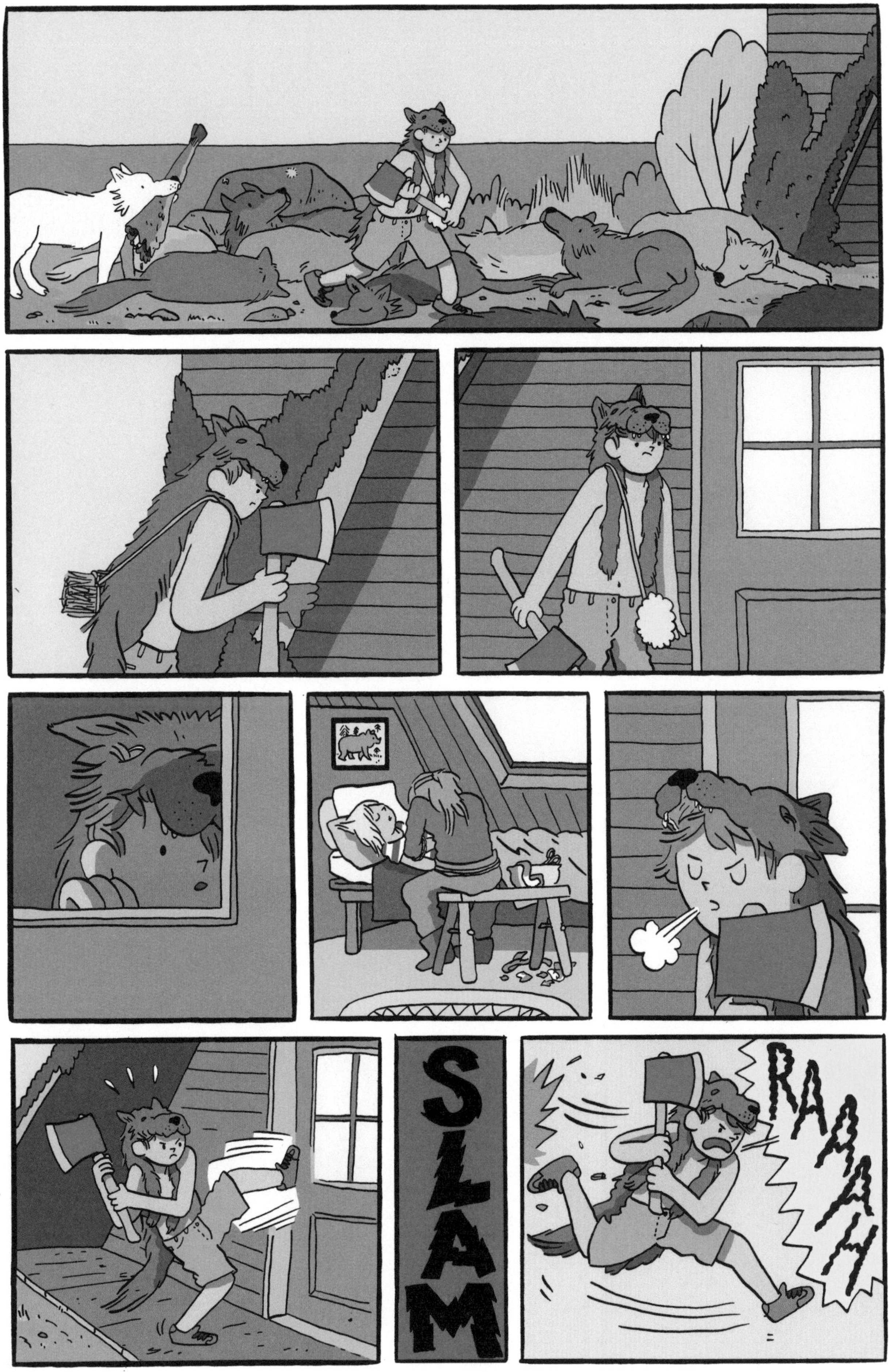
SLAM
RAAAAH

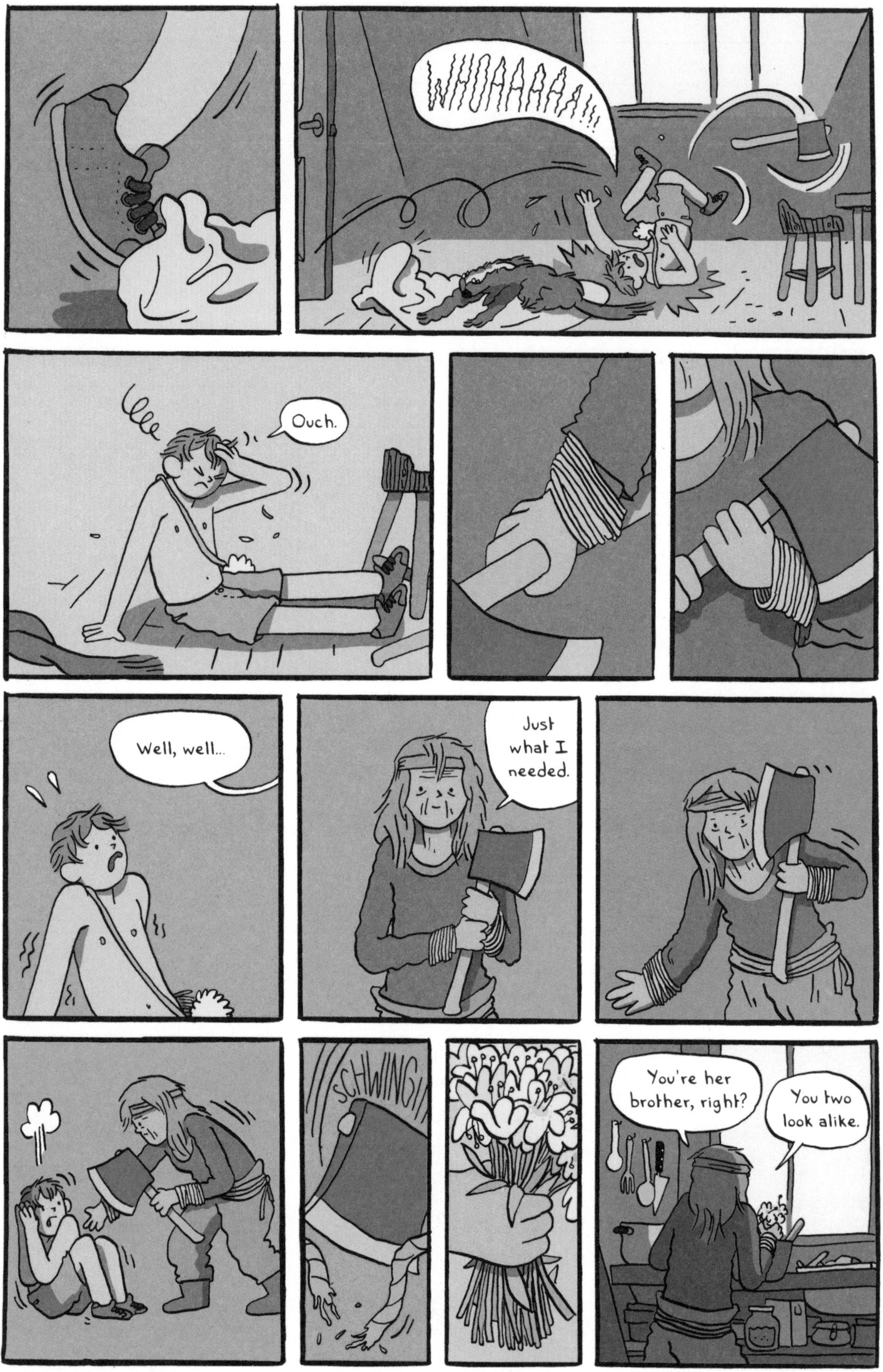
WHOAAAAAA!!!
Ouch.
Well, well...
Just what I needed.
SCHWING!!
You're her brother, right?
You two look alike.

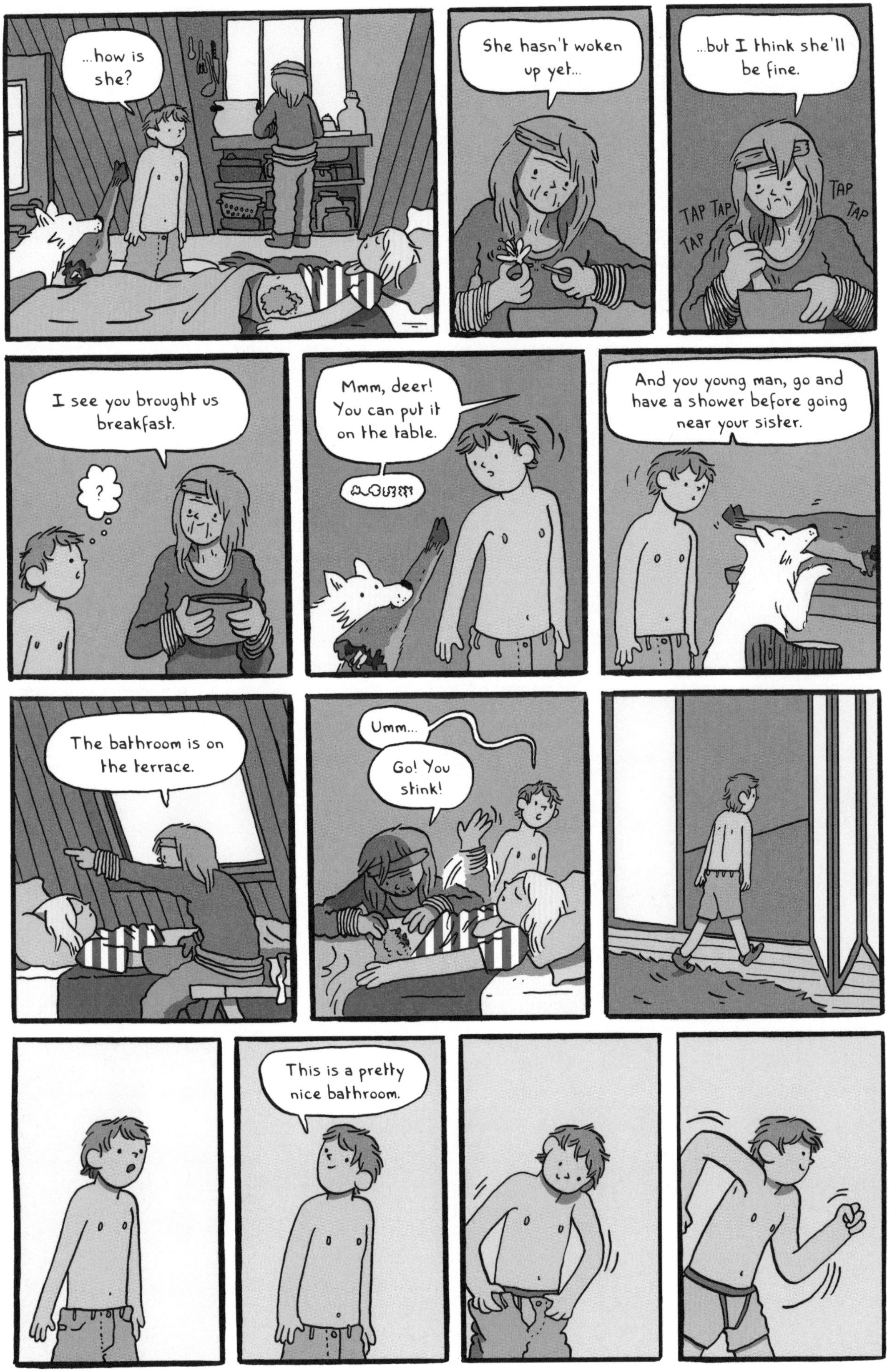
...how is she?
She hasn't woken up yet...
...but I think she'll be fine.
TAP TAP TAP
TAP TAP
I see you brought us breakfast.
?
Mmm, deer! You can put it on the table.
And you young man, go and have a shower before going near your sister.
The bathroom is on the terrace.
Umm...
Go! You stink!
This is a pretty nice bathroom.

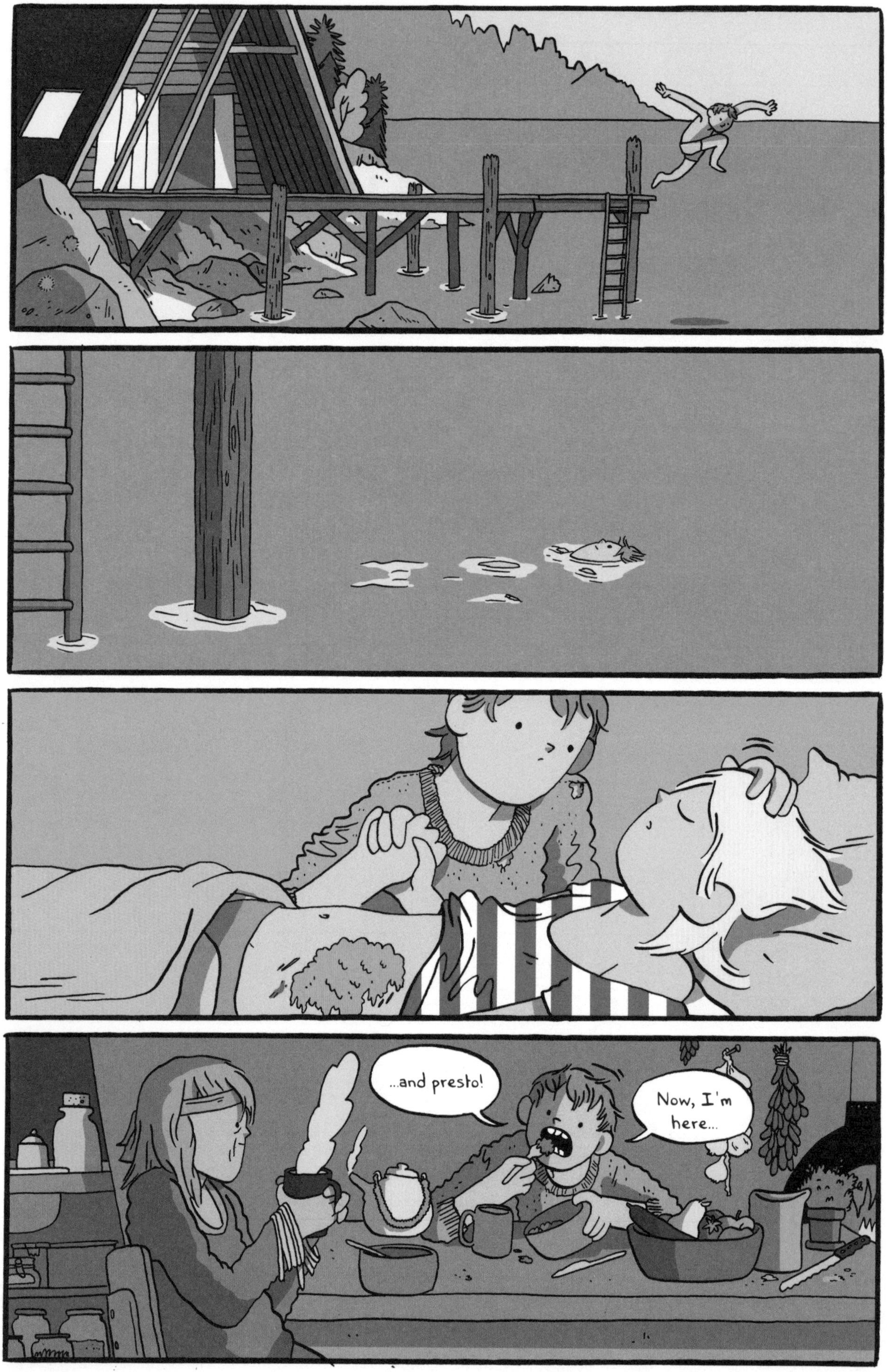
...and presto!
Now, I'm here...

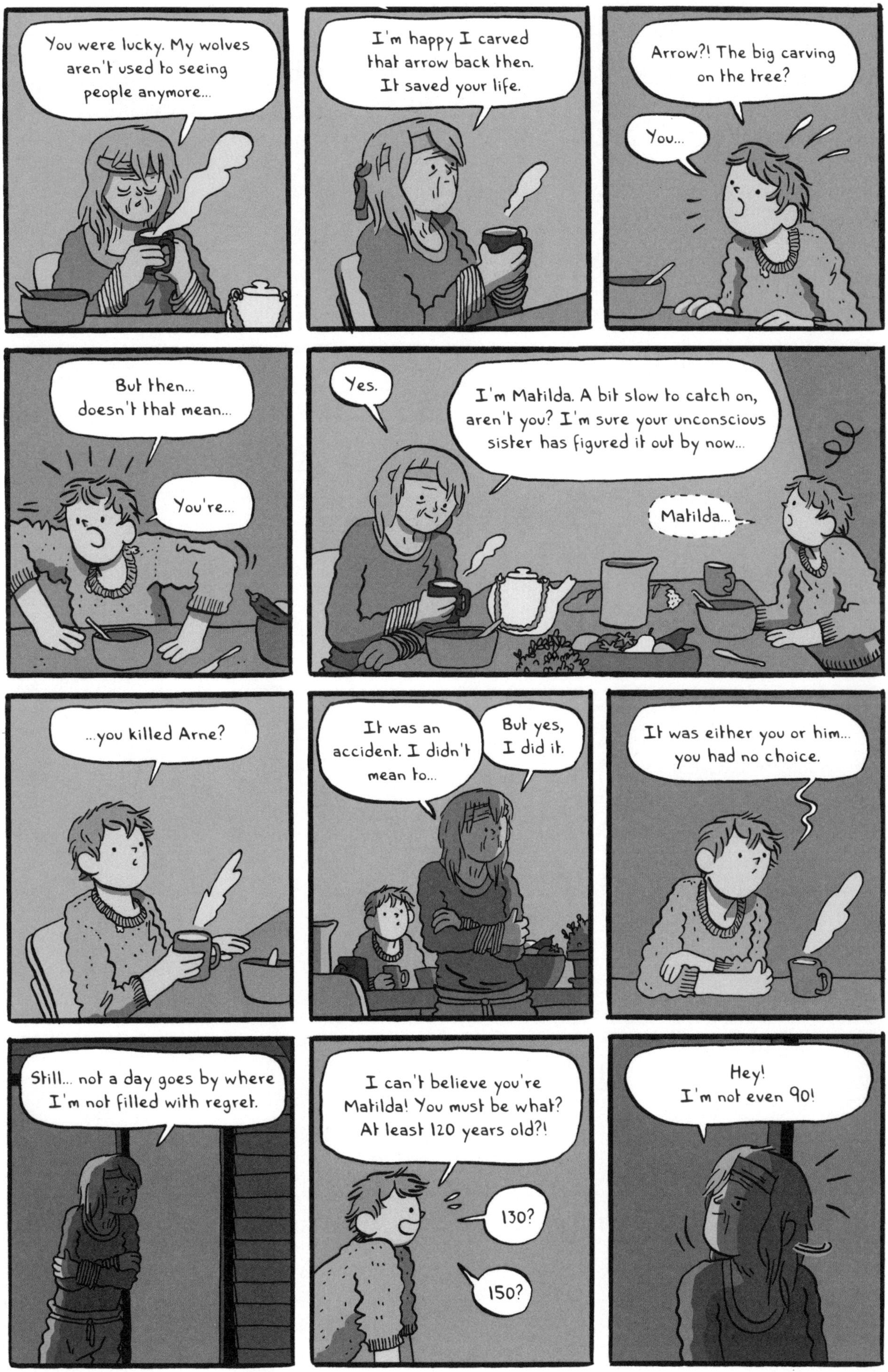
You were lucky. My wolves aren't used to seeing people anymore...
I'm happy I carved that arrow back then. It saved your life.
Arrow?! The big carving on the tree?
You...
But then... doesn't that mean...
You're...
Yes.
I'm Matilda. A bit slow to catch on, aren't you? I'm sure your unconscious sister has figured it out by now...
Matilda...
...you killed Arne?
It was an accident. I didn't mean to...
But yes, I did it.
It was either you or him... you had no choice.
Still... not a day goes by where I'm not filled with regret.
I can't believe you're Matilda! You must be what? At least 120 years old?!
130?
150?
Hey! I'm not even 90!

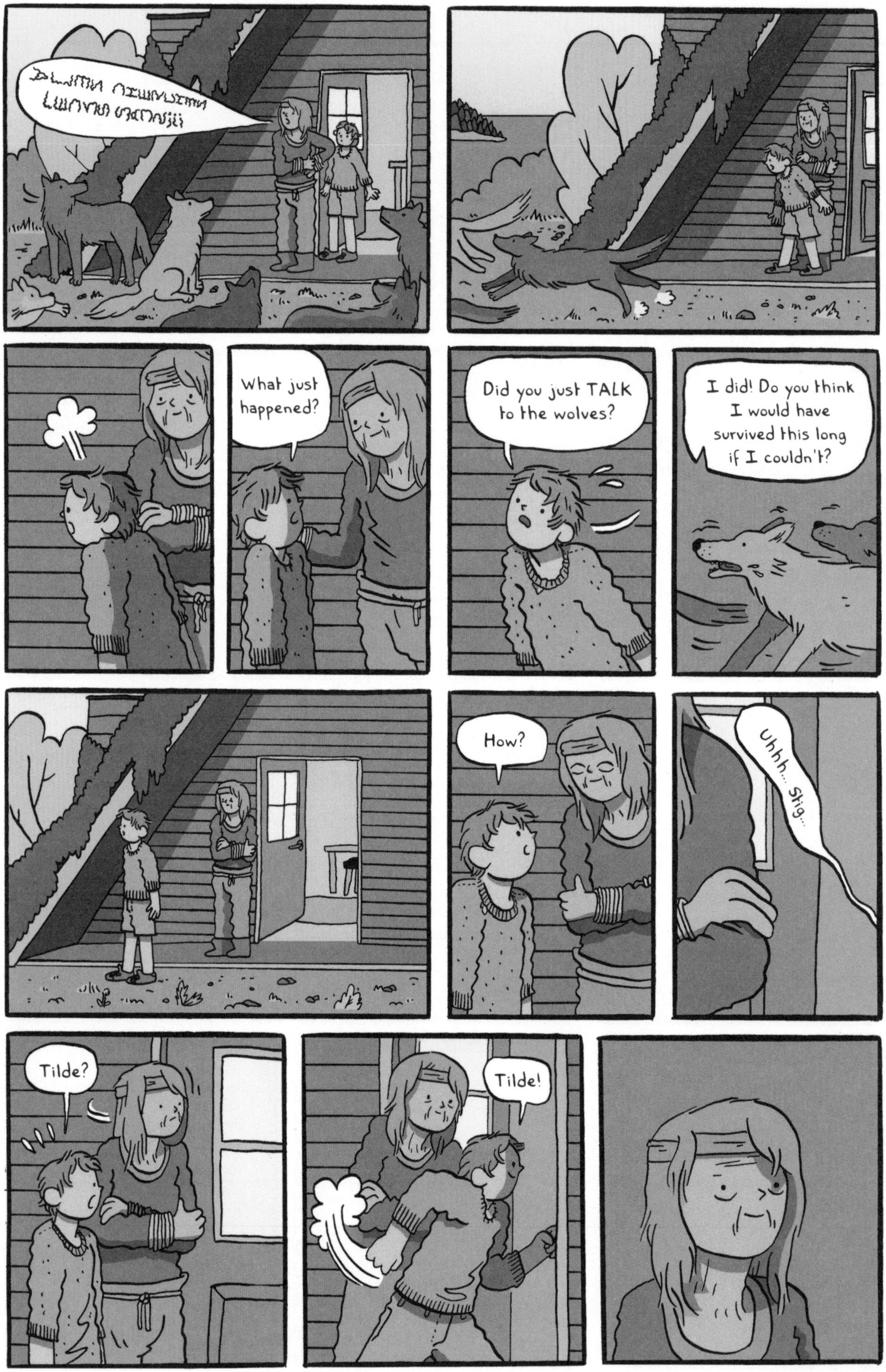
What just happened?
Did you just TALK to the wolves?
I did! Do you think I would have survived this long if I couldn't?
How?
Uhhh... Stig...
Tilde?
Tilde!

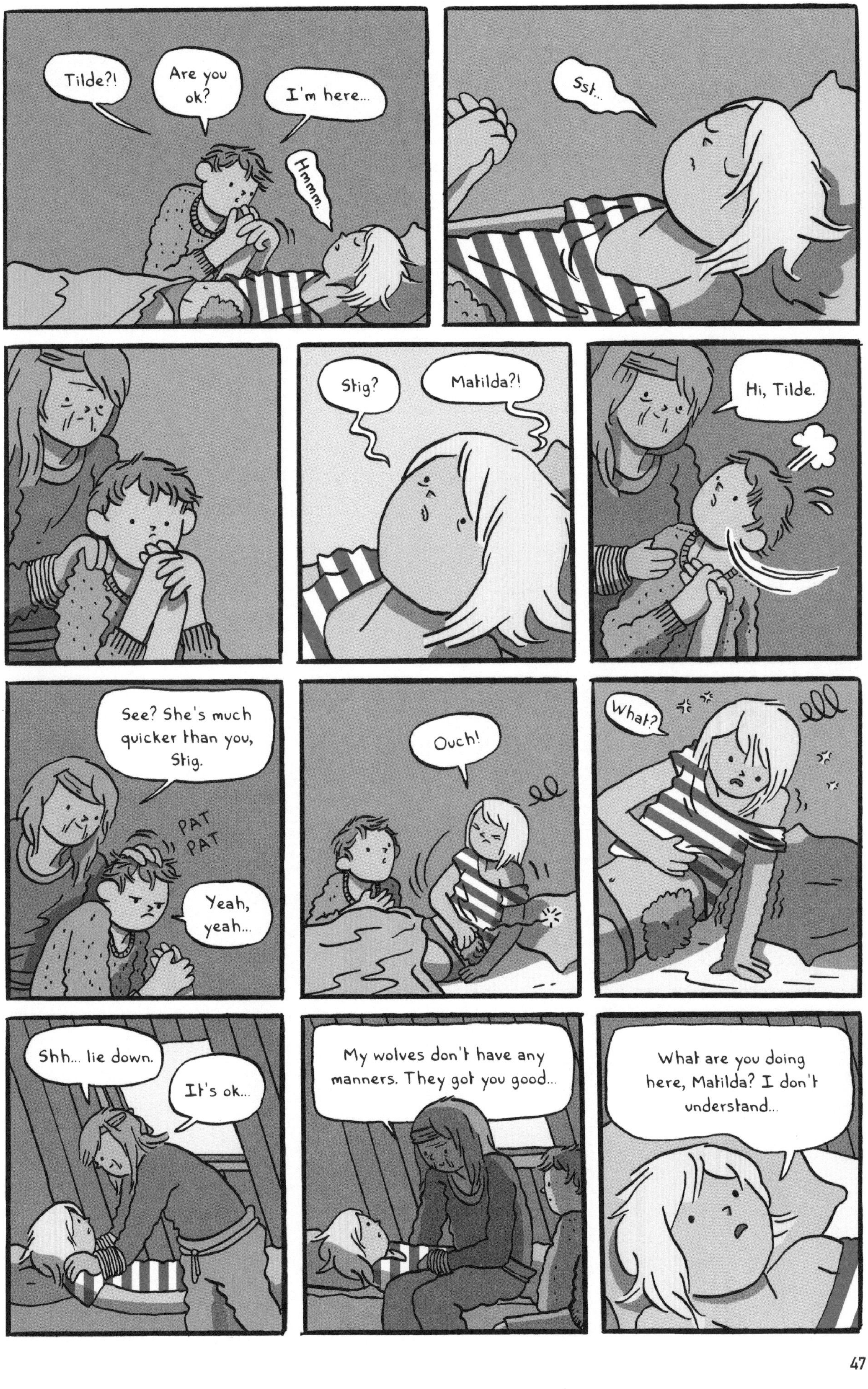
Tilde?!
Are you ok?
I'm here...
Hmmm.
Sst...
Stig?
Matilda?!
Hi, Tilde.
See? She's much quicker than you, Stig.
PAT PAT
Yeah, yeah...
Ouch!
What?
Shh... lie down.
It's ok...
My wolves don't have any manners. They got you good...
What are you doing here, Matilda? I don't understand...

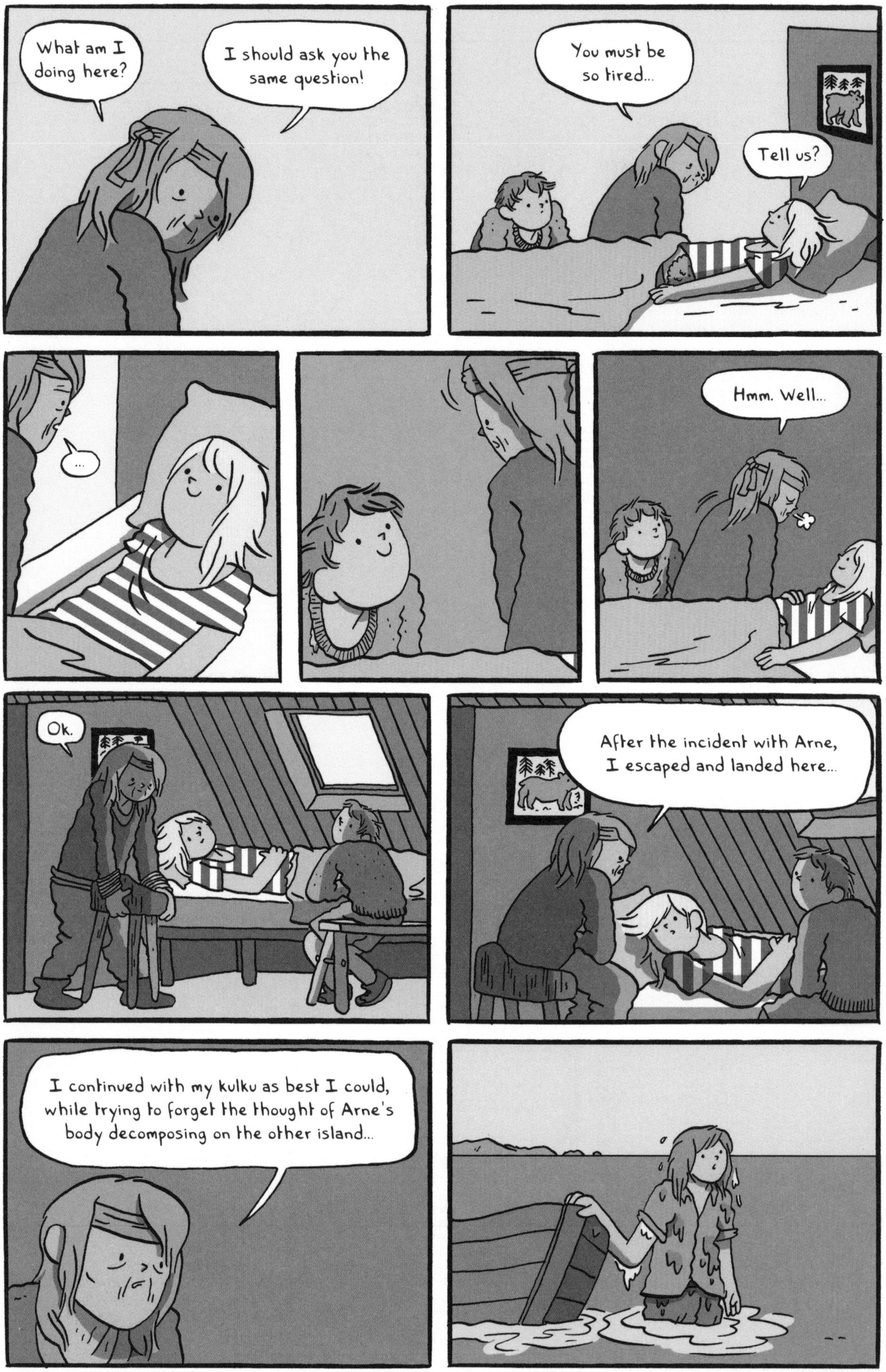
What am I doing here?
I should ask you the same question!
You must be so tired...
Tell us?
...
Hmm. Well...
Ok.
After the incident with Arne, I escaped and landed here...
I continued with my kulku as best I could, while trying to forget the thought of Arne's body decomposing on the other island...

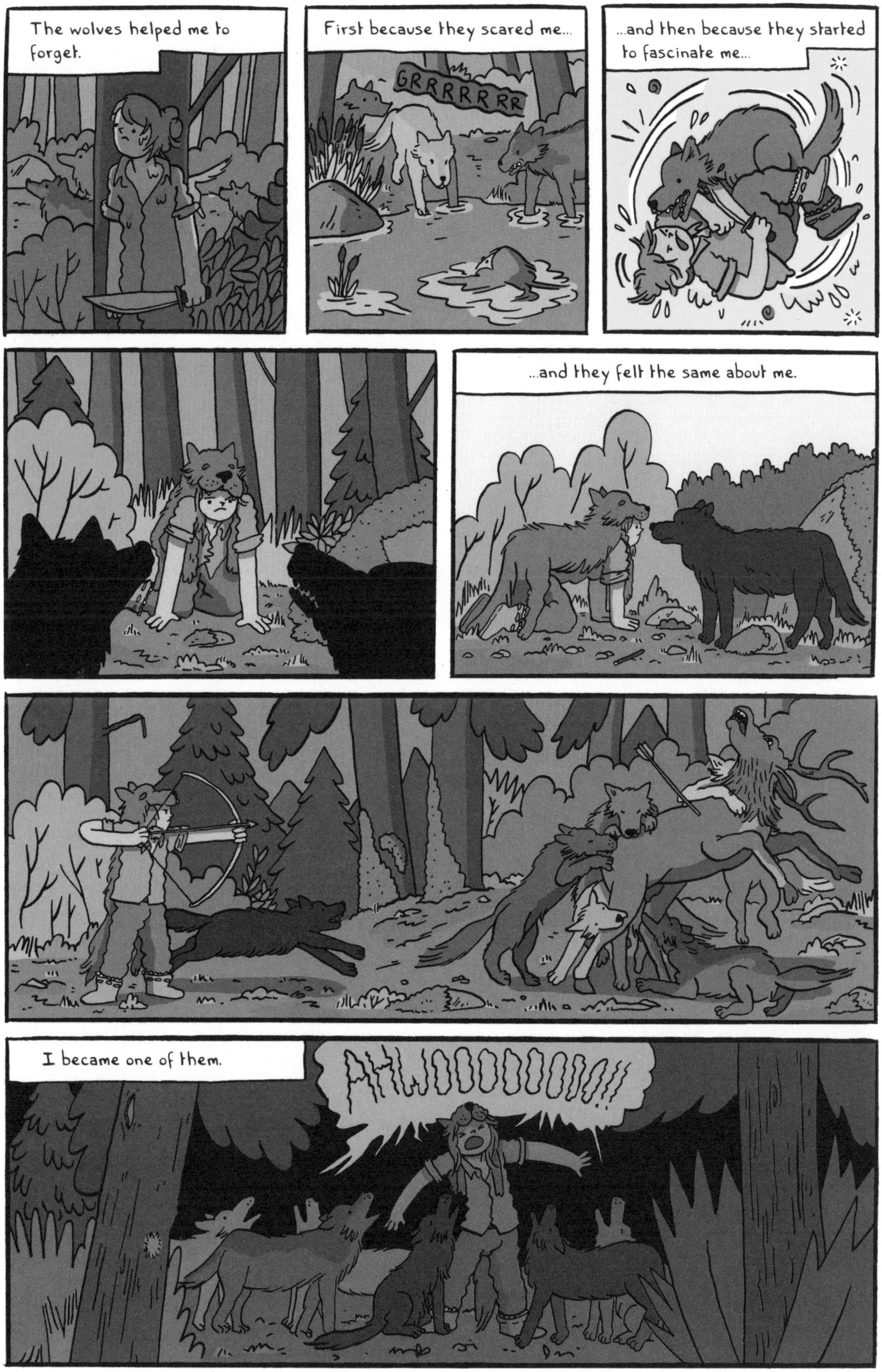
The wolves helped me to forget.
First because they scared me...
GRRRRRRRR
...and then because they started to fascinate me...
...and they felt the same about me.
I became one of them.
AHWOOOOOOOO!!

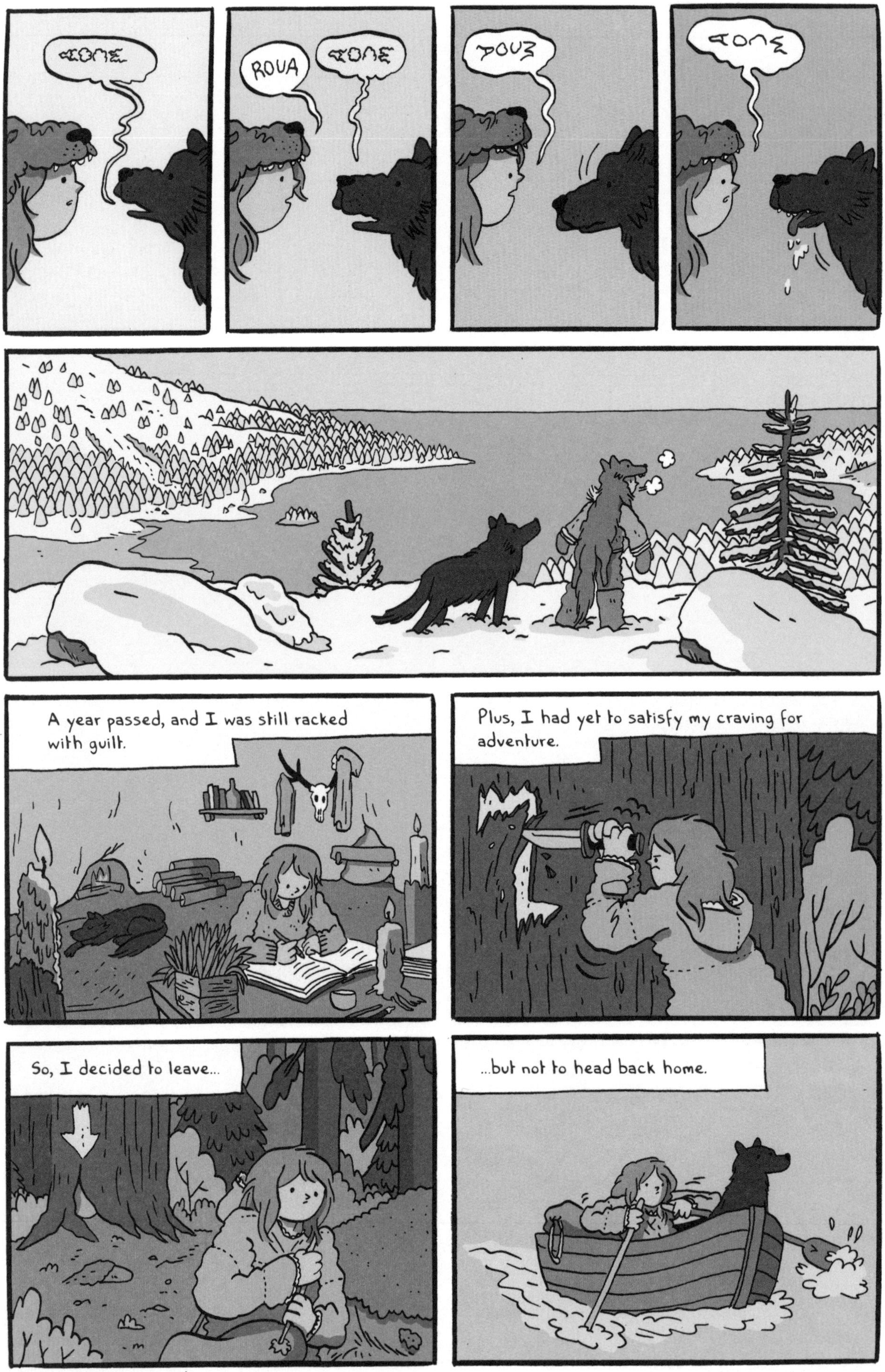
ROUA
A year passed, and I was still racked with guilt.
Plus, I had yet to satisfy my craving for adventure.
So, I decided to leave...
...but not to head back home.

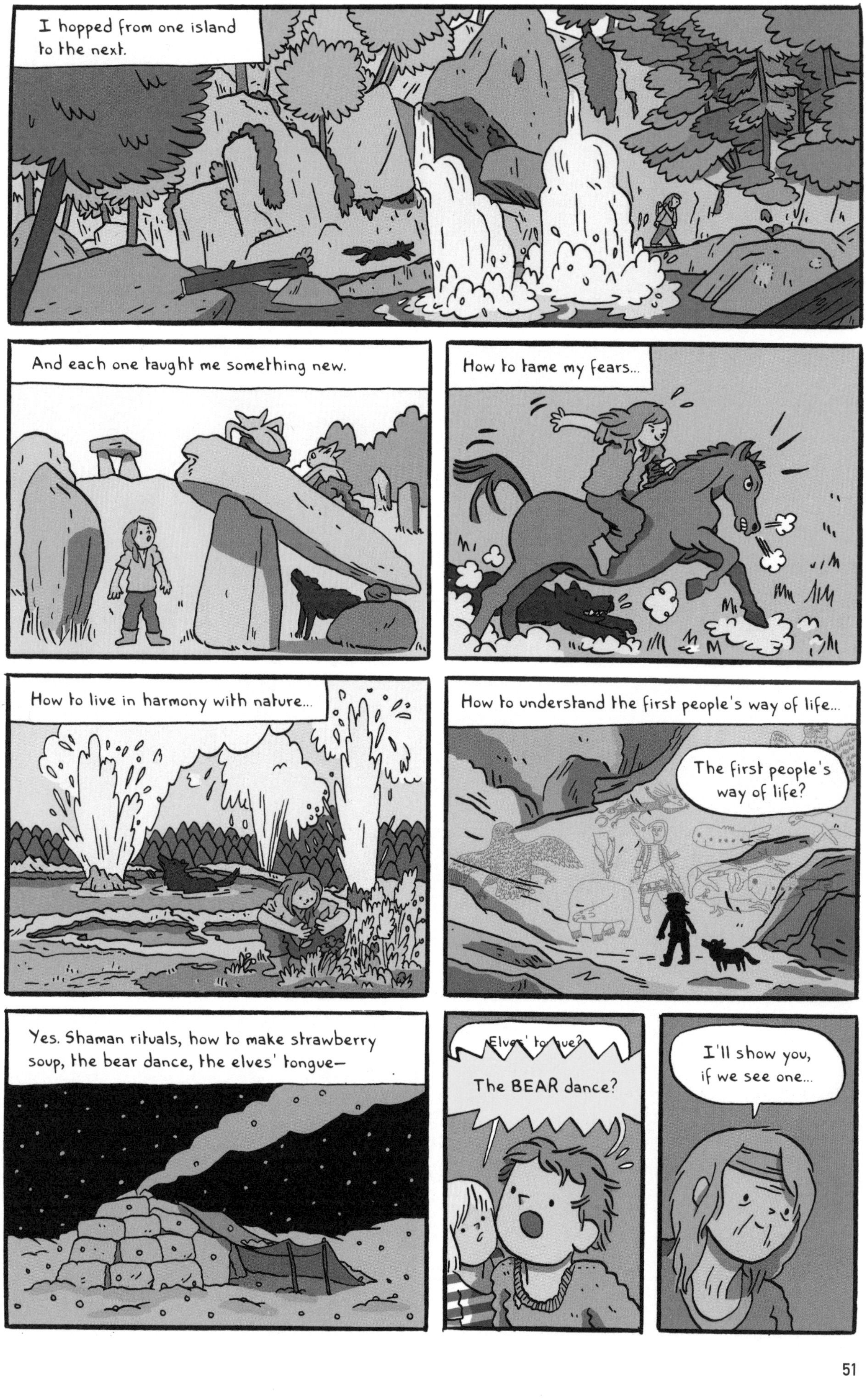
I hopped from one island to the next.
And each one taught me something new.
How to tame my fears...
How to live in harmony with nature...
How to understand the first people's way of life...
The first people's way of life?
Yes. Shaman rituals, how to make strawberry soup, the bear dance, the elves' tongue—
The BEAR dance?
I'll show you, if we see one...

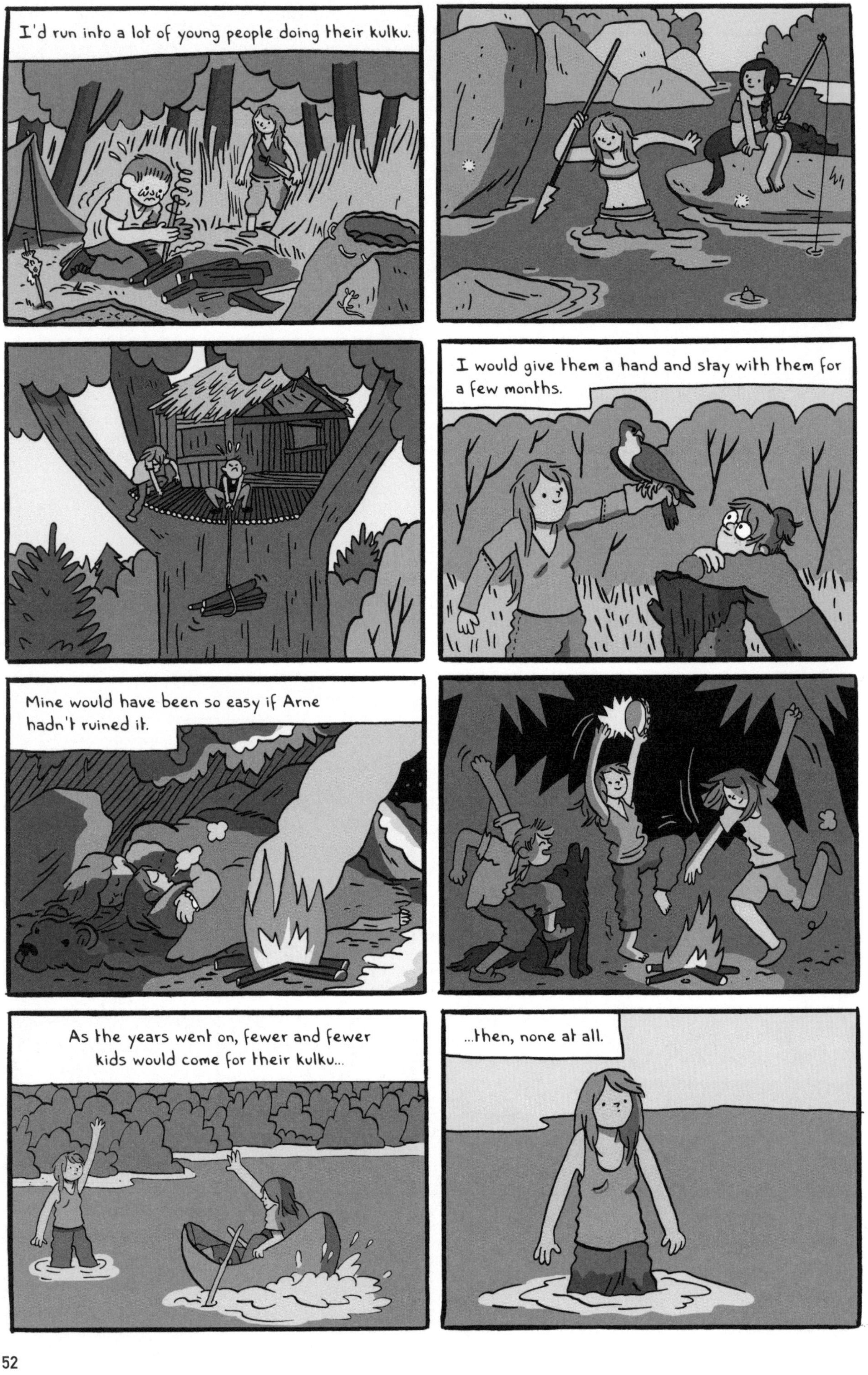
I'd run into a lot of young people doing their kulku.
I would give them a hand and stay with them for a few months.
Mine would have been so easy if Arne hadn't ruined it.
As the years went on, fewer and fewer kids would come for their kulku...
...then, none at all.

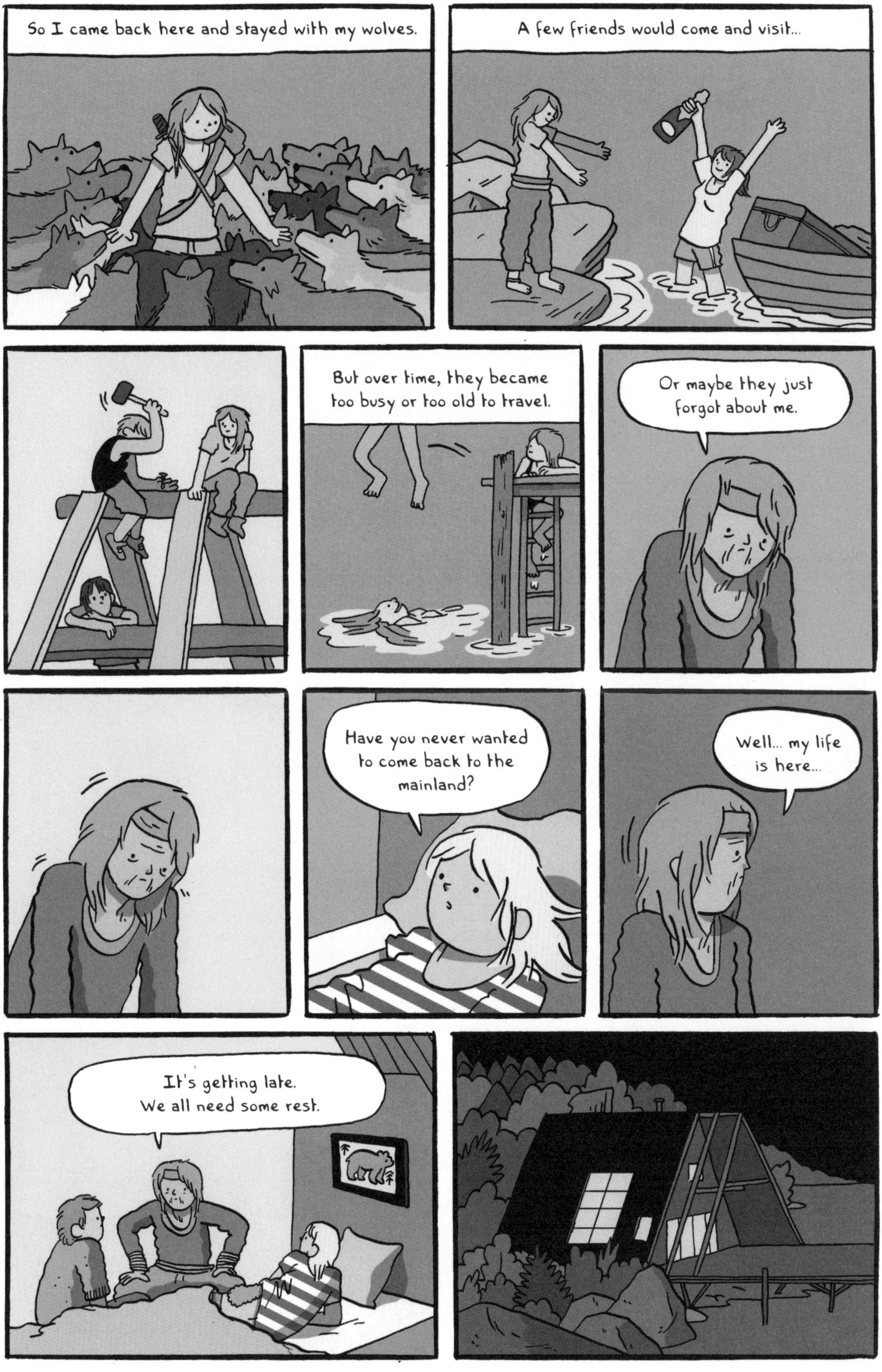

So I came back here and stayed with my wolves.
A few friends would come and visit...
But over time, they became too busy or too old to travel.
Or maybe they just forgot about me.
Have you never wanted to come back to the mainland?
Well... my life is here...
It's getting late. We all need some rest.

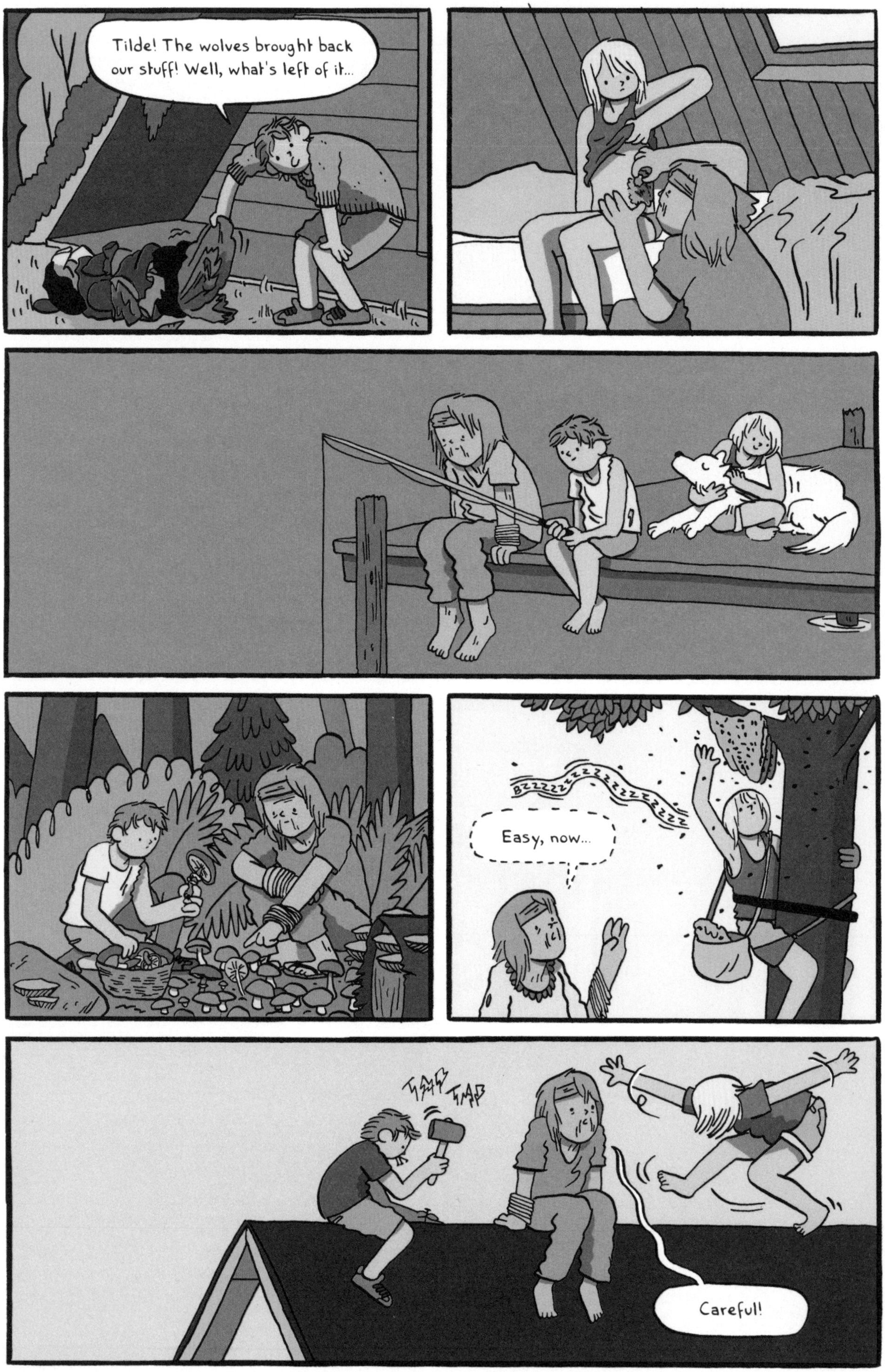
Tilde! The wolves brought back our stuff! Well, what's left of it...
BZZZZZZZZZZZZZZZZZZZ
Easy, now...
Careful!

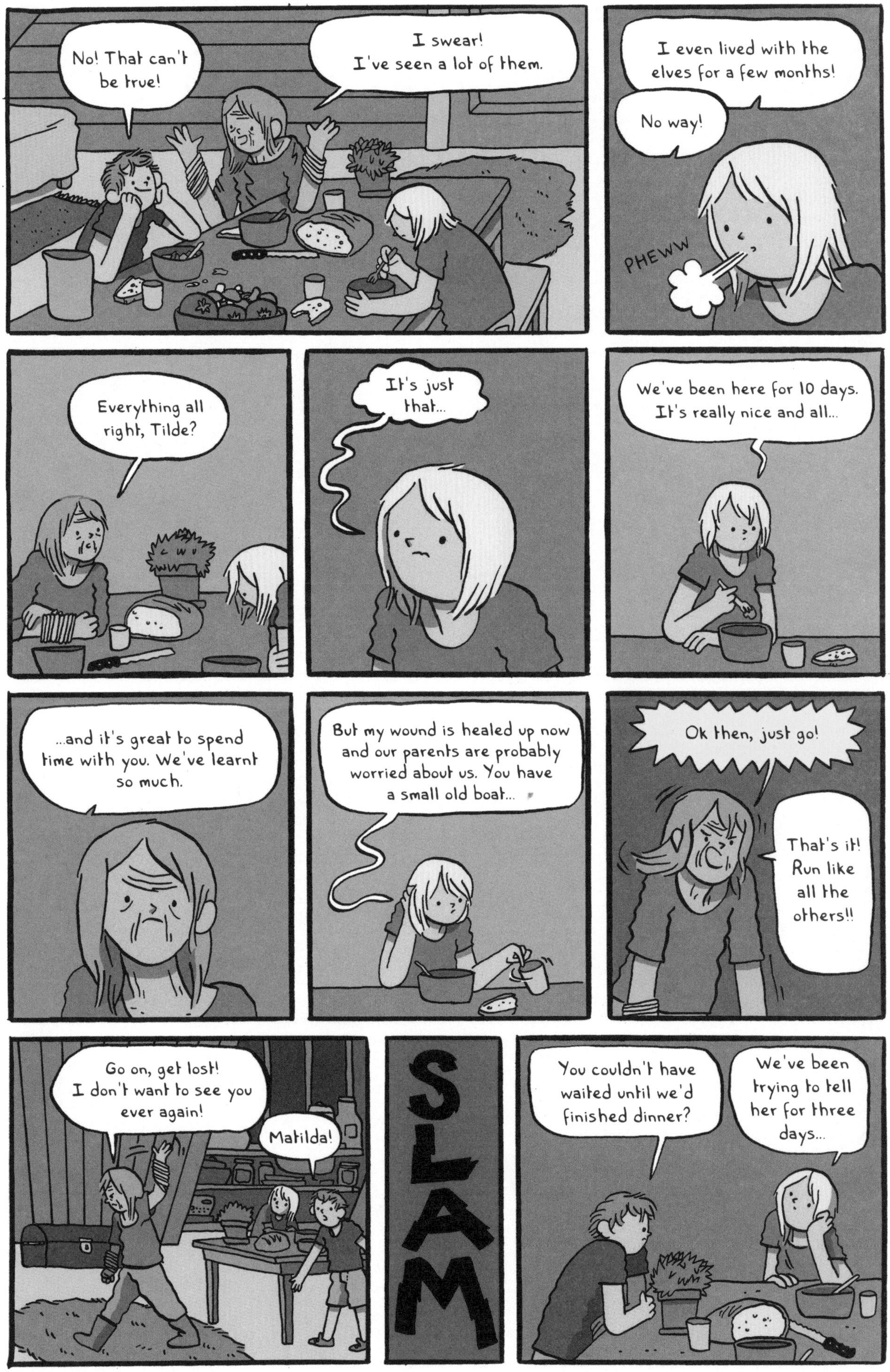
No! That can't be true!
I swear! I've seen a lot of them.
I even lived with the elves for a few months!
No way!
PHEWW
Everything all right, Tilde?
It's just that...
We've been here for 10 days. It's really nice and all...
...and it's great to spend time with you. We've learnt so much.
But my wound is healed up now and our parents are probably worried about us. You have a small old boat...
Ok then, just go!
That's it! Run like all the others!!
Go on, get lost! I don't want to see you ever again!
Matilda!
SLAM
You couldn't have waited until we'd finished dinner?
We've been trying to tell her for three days...

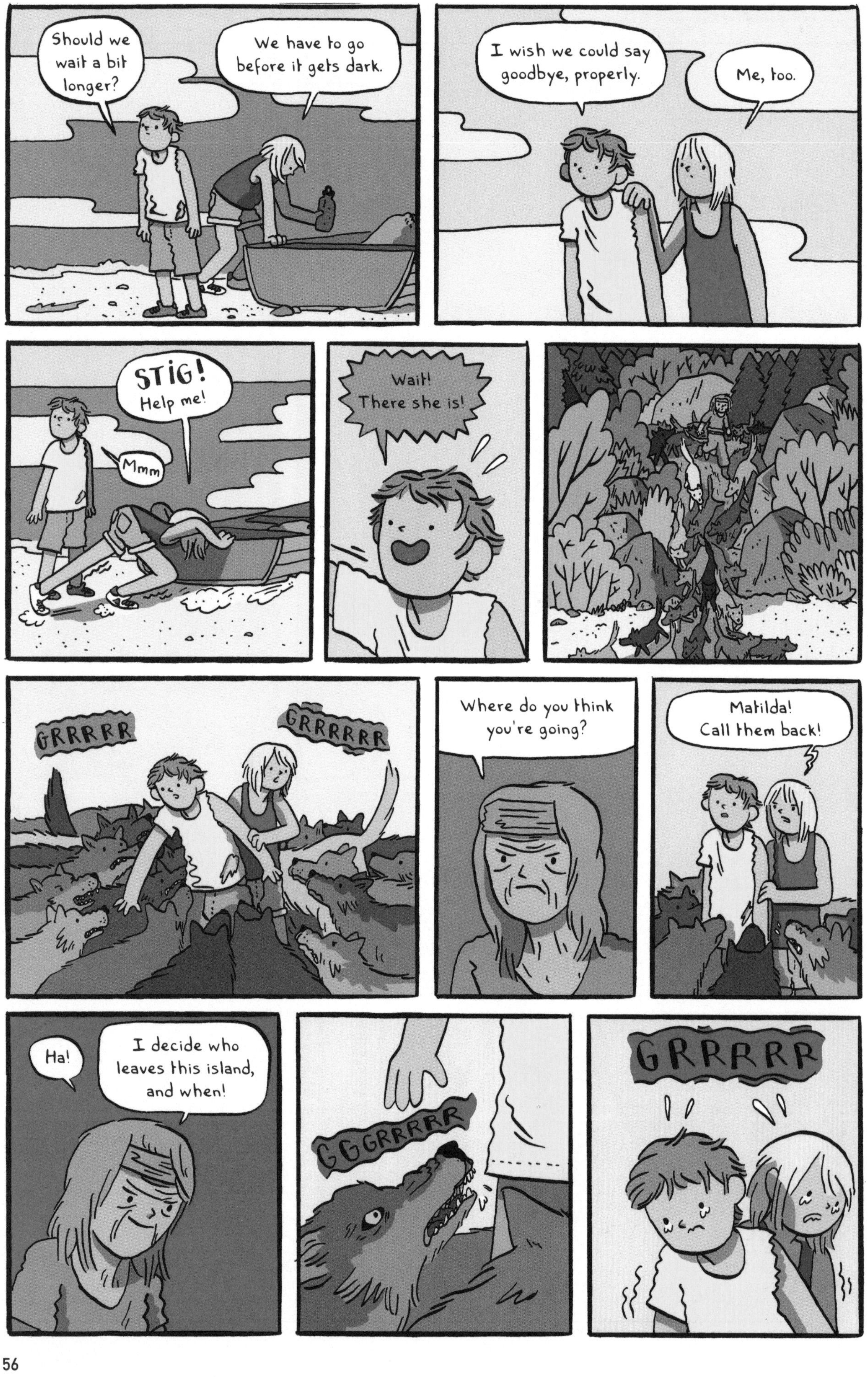
Should we wait a bit longer?
We have to go before it gets dark.
I wish we could say goodbye, properly.
Me, too.
STIG! Help me!
Mmm
Wait! There she is!
GRRRRR
GRRRRRR
Where do you think you're going?
Matilda! Call them back!
Ha!
I decide who leaves this island, and when!
GGGRRRRR
GRRRRR

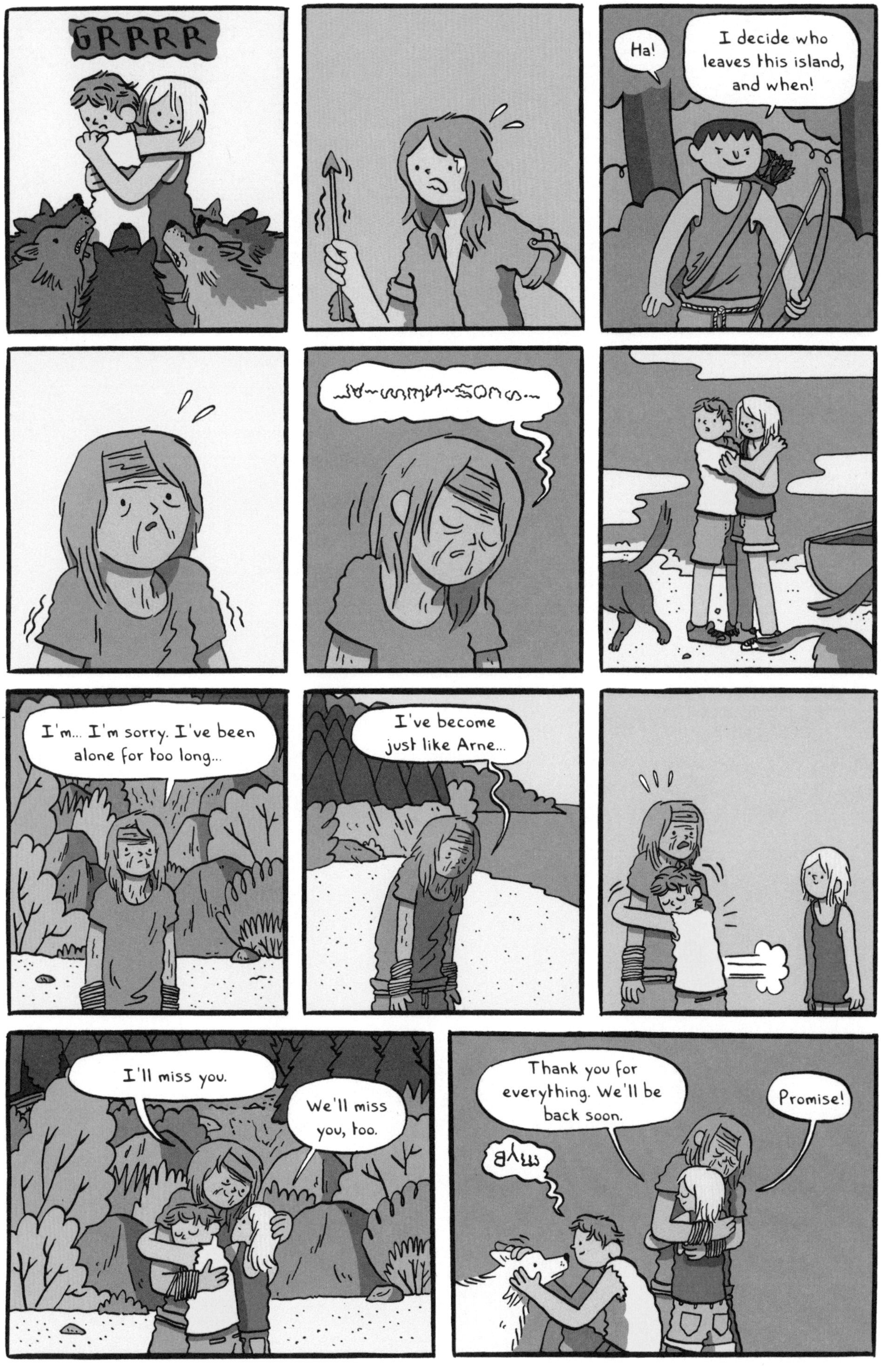
GRRRR
Ha!
I decide who leaves this island, and when!
I'm... I'm sorry. I've been alone for too long...
I've become just like Arne...
I'll miss you.
We'll miss you, too.
Thank you for everything. We'll be back soon.
Promise!

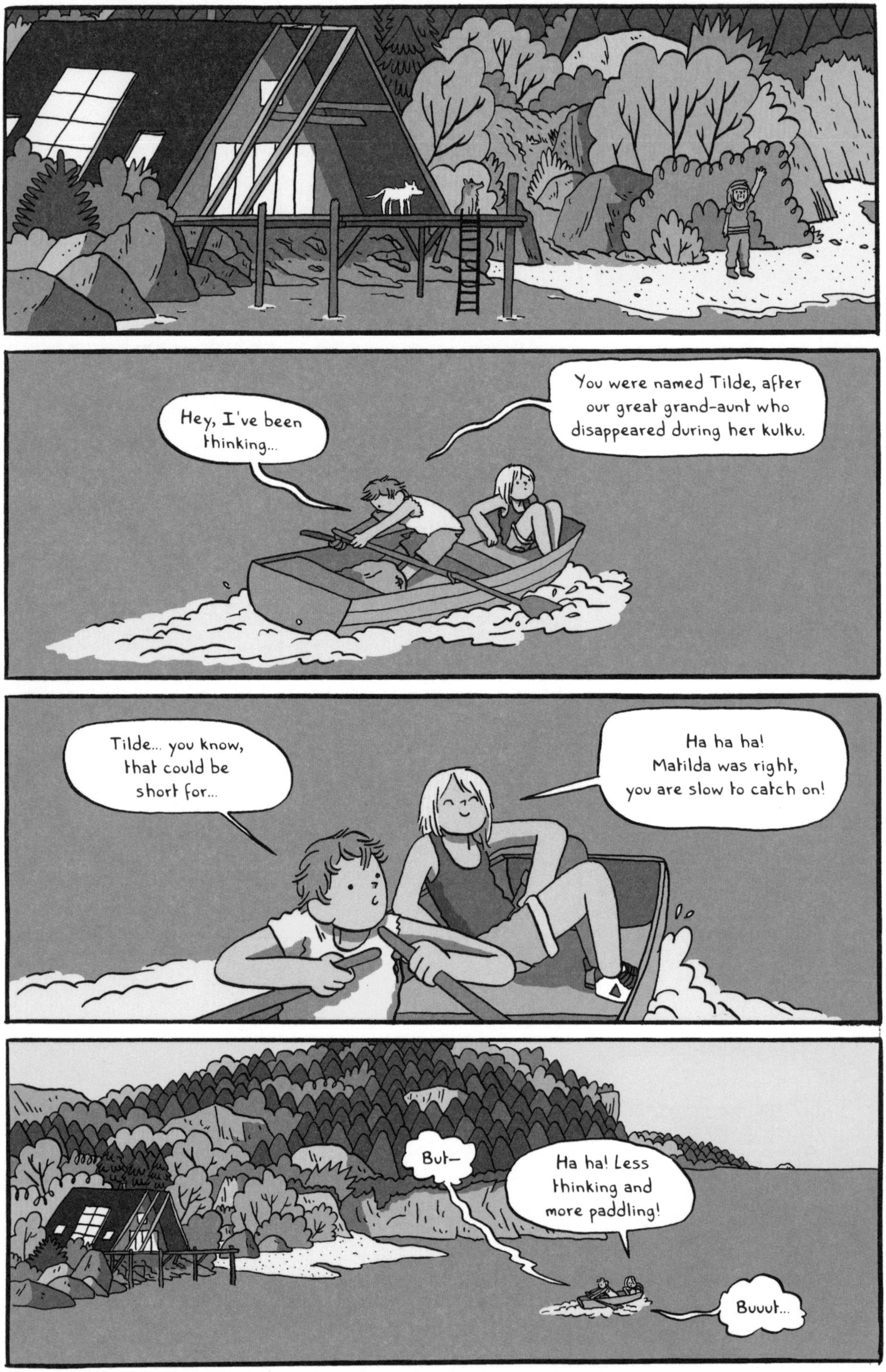
Hey, I've been thinking...
You were named Tilde, after our great grand-aunt who disappeared during her kulku.
Tilde... you know, that could be short for...
Ha ha ha! Matilda was right, you are slow to catch on!
But—
Ha ha! Less thinking and more paddling!
Buuut...

ABOUT THE AUTHOR

Max de Radiguès is a Belgian cartoonist and
publisher for L'employé Du Moi and Sarbacane.
His work is for both adults and children alike.

In September 2009, he was invited for a one-year
residency at the prestigious Center for Cartoon Studies
in White River Junction, USA. He recounted this year in his
book *Meanwhile In White River Junction*, which was part of
the official selection for the 2012 Angoulême International
Comics Festival. He currently lives in Brussels, Belgium.

COMING SOON:

STIG & TILDE
THE LOSER SQUAD

After one too many wrong turns, the twins finally arrive on the right island. Hot showers, wi-fi, all-day barbecue - this must be heaven! But there's trouble stirring on the island and maybe paradise isn't all it's cracked up to be. Can Stig and Tilde weather the storm one more time?

ISBN: 978-1-910620-66-3

First published in English in 2020 by Nobrow Ltd.
27 Westgate Street, London E8 3RL.

Stig & Tilde: Cheffe de meute, by Max de Radiguès © Éditions Sarbacane, France, 2018.

Published in agreement with Éditions Sarbacane through Sylvain Coissard Agency.

Text and illustrations by Max de Radiguès.

Translation by Marie Bédrune.

1 3 5 7 9 10 8 6 4 2

Published in the US by Nobrow (US) Inc.
Printed in Poland on FSC® certified paper.

ISBN: 978-1-910620-65-6
www.nobrow.net